I0547514

MURDER IN A SNOW COVERED TOWN
and other stories

By Eric Lee

Paragon Publishing
Professional Fiction Publisher
El Sobrante, California, USA

Author website: www.ericleestories.com

Copyright © 2008 by Paragon Publishing

Third Printing 2013

All rights reserved. No part of this book may be reproduced or utilized in any form or by any means, electronic or mechanical, including photocopying, recording, or by any information storage and retrieval system, without written permission from the author or the publisher.

For information address:

 Paragon Publishing
Professional Fiction Publisher
2300 Greenridge Drive
El Sobrante, California, 90274

Author website: www.ericleestories.com

Substantial discounts on bulk quantities of this author's publications are available to corporations, educational disciplines, professional associations, and other qualified organizations. For details and specific discount information, visit ericleestories.com and click on the "Contact Us" link at the bottom of the website. For more information about the author's stories, visit ericleestories.com

Printed in the United States of America

Murder in a Snow Covered Town and other stories
    Eric Lee
    Library of Congress Catalog Number: 2008927488 (first printing)
    ISBN: 978-0-9674476-3-6

Table of Contents

Dedication

For all of my family and friends
who have supported my writing

Special thanks to the following people who have helped me greatly in my writing:

Alexandria Chun
John Cmelak
Ellen Hanscom
Gary Kurtzman
Brian Lee
Clarence Lee
Gloria Lee
Damon Maxey
Jaelynn Mayes
Bill Raynolds
Mike Sutton
Patrick Sutton
Michael Wiley

Murder in a Snow Covered Town

My heart pounded rapidly and my hands trembled as I knocked on the door. Twenty years as a private investigator and meetings like this still give me a lump in my throat. I took off my brown hat and held it at my side. The porch awning shielded me from the light snowfall on this Sunday morning in December. Brian Flowers called me to his mansion-like home to investigate the disappearance of his ten-year-old daughter, who had been missing for the last two days.

I heard the barking, or what I would describe more like yapping, of a dog and then footsteps approaching the front door. The door opened and a middle aged man appeared. It was Brian Flowers.

A tall, imposing man with a muscular build, Brian was the president of a large advertising firm, founded by his father. Around town, the Flowers' name was synonymous with power, wealth, and success.

He had called me six months ago on another job, wanting me to spy on his wife because he suspected she was having an affair. I didn't find too much out. The best I could do was to take a relatively dark photo of his wife having drinks with another man in a hotel room. Unfortunately, the picture was too dark to recognize the man, and shortly thereafter, Brian notified me that my services were no longer needed.

"Spider, shut up!" Brian shouted at a yapping black and tan Dachshund. The dog responded by turning tail and running back into the house. "Sorry, it's my mother's dog. Barks at anything that moves. He's harmless though."

Brian motioned for me to come into the house and led me into the study. He picked up a scrapbook and opened it as he sat beside me on the couch. The anger and suspicion that I had sensed in him in the past had been replaced with grief and desperation. I could see it clearly on his face. He showed me a large picture of his daughter. A darling little girl with an award-winning smile, she had beautiful blond hair that fell down to her shoulders.

"This is Cindy. She's been missing since Friday."

"What do you know about how she spent her Friday?"

"The police checked with her teacher, she was at school all day." He didn't look at me while talking. Instead, he stared at Cindy's picture, which was resting on his lap. "And I talked to Cindy's best friend, Serena. She said..."

"How old is Serena?"

"She's ten also," Brian replied, still looking at the picture of Cindy. "She said that she had walked home with Cindy Friday afternoon and watched her go into this house. And that's the last anyone ever saw of her."

"What time was that?"

"School ends at 2:15. It's about a fifteen-minute walk from the school. So, about 2:30."

"So, there was no one else in the house at that time?"

"No," Brian said, looking up at me. "Linda and I were working. My mother was at the community center all afternoon. And my fifteen year old son, Matthew, was at basketball practice."

"Did Cindy always come home to an empty house?"

"Sometimes. Linda works part-time so she's home on Tuesdays and Thursdays. On the other days, well, we felt that Cindy was old enough to take care of herself."

"Apparently not," I thought.

"She's a very mature ten year old," Brian said, reading the expression on my face. "Three months ago, she won Junior Miss America. For the contest, each child must show some talent. She'd come home and practice her magic act."

"When did someone realize Cindy was missing?"

"I think my mother was the first to come home, then Matthew. I got home from work a little after five o'clock. When Matthew told me that he hadn't seen her, I called Linda at work. She said she wasn't with her and I knew something was wrong."

We quickly discussed my fee, which included a $20,000 bonus if I found Cindy alive. It was all on a one page contract Brian had drawn up. $20,000 was some incentive. Money was certainly no obstacle to Brian when it came to finding his daughter. He gave me his cell phone number and told me to call him if I found out anything important.

He gave me a firm handshake and looked me straight in the eye. "I'm counting on you to find my daughter. She means everything to me." He told me that he had to go to a neighborhood watch meeting, but he said I could talk to anyone in the house. He led me upstairs to Alice's room. Her room, which was very spacious, had several paintings and a porcelain crucifix on the wall. It was meticulously clean with each pillow lying perfectly in place on the bed. Brian introduced me to his mother, Alice, referring to me as "the gentleman who was going to find Cindy."

Alice sat in a large armchair near her bed. She appeared to be in her mid eighties. Her face was lined with wrinkles and her hair was completely white. She wore thick, gold colored eyeglasses. Less noticeable was a small, white hearing aid in her right ear. She held a cane in one hand and rubbed her dog's back with the other. I walked over to her to shake her hand. I was surprised. I expected her to be weak and frail, but instead her handshake was quite firm and powerful.

"I have to leave now, but Robert is going to stay and talk to you." He bent down to hug his mother before leaving.

There was a momentary silence as we just looked at each other. "Is this your dog?" I asked as I sat down on the edge of the bed.

"Why yes," she said with a smile. The Dachshund was chewing on a rawhide bone. "He's a great companion. Stays with me all the time."

"Brian tells me you were at the community center Friday afternoon. Did Spider go with you?"

"Heavens no. Dogs aren't allowed at the center. He stayed here."

"Does he stay inside or outside when you're gone?"

"Well, he has a little doggie door so he can be in either place, but he usually prefers the house."

"When did you get back from the center last Friday?"

"I don't know. 'Bout four thirty, I'd guess."

"And Cindy wasn't home when you returned?"

"I don't know. I mean I don't think so," Alice said, stumbling over her own words. "I was tired. I didn't look for her. I just went straight to my room to take a nap."

"So do you have any idea what happened to Cindy? Any idea where she might be?"

Alice slowly rose from her chair, causing Spider to leap to the ground. She slowly walked with her cane toward the bedroom window. "Cindy will be back." She reached down to pick up a necklace, which prominently displayed a crucifix. She held the cross close to her bosom. "God will show Cindy the way home."

I dropped my head, realizing this ordeal must be tough on her. "Did you notice Cindy upset or unhappy at all last week? Any indication that she might want to run away from home?"

Alice turned around to face me. The endearing smile was gone from her face. It was replaced by a glare. It startled me. "Cindy was a happy child. She was a Miss America. She didn't run away. Some evil force took her, probably the devil." She turned around to look outside again before saying in a softer, friendlier tone, "She'll find her way home. God will show her the way."

I decided that I had obtained all of the relevant information that I could from Alice. She pointed me toward Matthew's room. I walked down the hallway and opened the second door. A startled boy sat in a chair next to an open window. Wearing a tee shirt and faded blue jeans, he held a lit cigarette in his hand.

"Hey, you ever heard of knockin'?"

"I'm sorry," I said, entering the room and closing the door behind me. He continued to smoke as I sat on the unmade bed near him. The room, littered with clothes and sports equipment, was a stark contrast to Alice's pristine bedroom. "Does your dad know you smoke?" He shook his head as he glared at me, probably still upset with the intrusion. "My name is Robert," I said, extending my hand. "I'm a private invest...."

"What do you want?"

I put down my hand, which was awkwardly hanging out there. "I want to find your sister."

"Everything is always about her, the golden child. When she was here, she had the spotlight. Now that she's gone, she still has it."

"Surely, you want someone to find your sister?"

He looked me straight in the eye for about five seconds before finally saying, "Of course."

11

"Good, I just have a few questions for you," I said, pulling out my notepad. "When did you get home from school last Friday?"

"I don't know," he said before exhaling smoke. "I had basketball practice so I probably got home around five o'clock."

"When you get home on the weekdays, is Cindy usually there?"

"Usually."

"So you were surprised when Cindy wasn't home?"

"No. I just figured my dad or Linda came home early to take her some place. You know, magic lessons or singing lessons, whatever."

"Was Cindy unhappy at all before her disappearance?"

"Unhappy? Give me a break. What did she have to be unhappy about? She was perfect. Dad drooled over her. Linda always took her side. Grandma couldn't stop talking about her. Everybody loved her."

"What about you?" I asked with raised eyebrows. "Did you love her?"

Matthew glared at me again before jamming what was left of his cigarette into an ashtray that was resting on the windowsill. "I'm going to shoot some hoops. I have a big game tonight. The team is counting on me."

I took Matthew's not so subtle hint and left his room. I decided to take a quick tour of the house. It was a beautiful house: two stories, five bedrooms upstairs, a living room, a dining room, a study, a large kitchen, and another large entertainment room downstairs in addition to a large backyard.

I was coming back into the house when an attractive woman appearing to be in her early forties greeted me. I figured the woman was Brian's wife. The woman was tall with long blond hair. She had draped herself in jewelry- earrings, bracelet, and an extravagant necklace. I would guess her clear beauty on the outside masked the pain, desperation, and emptiness she felt inside with her only daughter missing.

We introduced ourselves and walked into the living room and sat down. She said that she last saw Cindy Friday morning when she helped her get ready for school.

"Any reason you can think of why Cindy might run away?" I asked as delicately as possible. "I mean, was she depressed or upset at all?"

"No, not at all. She was a very happy child. She would never run away from home."

"You and your husband are very well known and wealthy. Do you think someone took her for ransom money?"

"Maybe, but we haven't gotten any call, note, anything from anyone who might have kidnapped her. It's been two days." Linda pulled out a tissue from her purse to wipe her eyes.

Unfortunately, Linda was right. She would have been contacted if Cindy had been abducted for ransom money. And if Cindy didn't run away from home, all of the other possibilities lead to a scenario where it was not likely she would be found alive.

Linda got up from her chair. She opened up a nearby cabinet, revealing rows and rows of videotapes. "I want you to take a couple of videotapes of Cindy. They're mostly stuff we taped that we thought we might send to a talent agent. I want you to know my daughter. Not a minute goes by when I'm not thinking about where she is. The thought of my little baby with some stranger doing God knows what!" Linda paused as she covered her face with her left hand. Moments later, she had composed herself, removing her left hand from her face and giving me the two videotapes with her right hand. "You look at these tapes and then find my daughter."

I left the house and headed for the local police station. I have lived in this town for over fifteen years. And during that time, I always worked hard to develop a strong relationship with the police department.

The result of my labor is a bonafide friendship with the senior deputy Riley Lawton. Riley and I fish together on occasion. I think Riley and I got along so well because we were both bachelors, neither of us ever able to locate Ms. Right. When it was appropriate, Riley didn't mind confiding in me on a particular case I was working on. Riley's daily donut craving was partially the cause for him being slightly overweight. But, he still was a healthy, handsome man. Riley sported stylish eye-glasses which made him look distinguished. Like me, Riley was in his fifties, but was still a kid at heart. He almost always had a pleasant disposition and great interpersonal skills. For the last nine years, he earned the trust and confidence of the public.

Unfortunately, I didn't have a good relationship with the sheriff, a Mister Larry Metzger. Although he was a young man in his mid thirties, Metzger had been in law enforcement since he was twenty one. He was promoted to sheriff a year ago when he was transferred to our small town. I think he saw me as a nuisance and a meddler.

When I entered the police station, Riley gave me a warm greeting and I sat down in front of his desk in an open area of the station. Being a Sunday, the station was quiet. "So what brings you down here?" Riley asked before taking a sip from his coffee.

"The Cindy Flowers case. Mr. Flowers hired me to find her."

"I see. So, you're employed by the wealthiest, most powerful man in town. Tell me. What's he paying you?"

"The usual hourly rate," I said calmly before smiling. "Plus $20,000 if I find Cindy alive." Riley whistled which showed me he was impressed. "So, what can you tell me about the police investigation to find her?"

"Well, technically nothing," Riley said with a smile.

"Come on."

"All kidding aside. I want to find that girl as badly as you do. She's a darling, little kid. I met her a couple of times. You know, she won Junior Miss America."

"So I keep hearing."

"I'll tell you one thing. If I had to guess, I'd say Cindy ran away from home."

"Why do you say that?"

"Cindy's parents pushed her to be the best at everything. That's a lot of pressure to put on a ten year old. She probably had enough."

"I don't know," I said, shaking my head. "Seems to me that Cindy's parents are more neglectful than anything else. Most weekdays Cindy comes home to an empty house."

"Whether it's overbearing or neglect, either would be reasons for Cindy to run away."

"True, but I talked to the whole family earlier today. They said she was very happy leading up to her disappearance."

"A bit of advice for you," Riley said chuckling. "Don't believe a word anyone says in that household. They've all got something wrong with them."

"What do you mean?"

"Well, the son, what's his name, uh.. Matthew has been hauled down here so many times I've lost count."

"What did Matthew do?"

"Well, let's see," Riley said, leaning back in his chair and holding his fingers out as if to count. "One time he was caught shoplifting. Another time bloodied some kid nose in a fight right in front of the police station. Another time he broke into the school cafeteria." Riley snickered. "His defense was he was hungry."

"What can you tell me about Matthew's grandmother, Alice?"

"Crazy as a loon," Riley said as he twirled his index finger around his right ear. "I've met her a few times when there was some kind of disturbance at the Flowers' house. I drive all the way down there and when I ask Alice what happened, she just says 'Hear no evil. See no evil. But God hears all and sees all'."

"Wait a minute. What kind of disturbance?"

"Well, we usually get a call from neighbors. They hear a lot of yelling. It's always some kind of domestic dispute between Mr. and Mrs. Flowers. That Mr. Flowers has quite a temper. Twice when I came down, Mrs. Flowers had bruises on her face and arms. I think Mr. Flowers hit her."

"Did you arrest him?"

"Naw, because Mrs. Flowers always made up some stupid story saying that she got the bruises from a fall," Riley said. "She refused to press charges. And to me, that makes her the sickest of the bunch."

"You could've brought charges on him based on the physical evidence. I mean, bruises from a fall are different from bruises from physical abuse. You could have proven that in court."

"It's not that simple. Brian Flowers is rich and powerful. He'd hire a truckload of lawyers. His wife would get on the stand and swear that Brian didn't do anything. And when we lost, Brian would launch a massive civil suit for wrongful arrest." I sat back in my chair astonished.

"Well, well, look what the cat dragged in," a voice said from behind me. I turned around and saw Sheriff Metzger. With a boyish face that was devoid of facial hair, Metzger simply looked too young to be wearing a sheriff's uniform. I always felt Metzger tried to compensate for his "baby face looks" by being an overbearing, intimidating dictator in a vain attempt to prove he deserved the position. He was a tall, buff man who liked to spend his free time in the local gym. He was wearing a blue hat which hid most of his wavy, black hair. Everything about Metzger reeked of arrogance. His strut, his sinister grin, his hands on his hips, and his condescending voice. "So what brings you in here?"

"I was hired to find Cindy Flowers. I thought we could both benefit from each other's involvement. After all, what really matters is that Cindy is found alive, right sheriff?"

"Listen to me and listen good," Metzger said. "I don't need your help and when we help you, it only slows us down. I don't want you taking up my deputy's time to discuss this case. You got that?"

I looked over to Riley who simply shook his head, which I read as a sign to leave. "Yeah, I got it," I said as I walked toward the exit. At the doorway, I turned around and said to the sheriff, "It would be pretty embarrassing for you if I find Cindy before you do. And you had a two day head start."

After leaving the police station, I set up a meeting with Serena, Cindy's friend and the last person that claims to have seen Cindy. When I drove to Serena's house, very light snow flurries filled the cool air. The small flurries quickly melted when they hit the ground. When I pulled up to the house, it was a little after two o'clock in the afternoon, nearly 48 hours since Cindy's disappearance.

Serena's mom invited me in and we sat down with Serena in the living room. Serena had curly brown hair, which was tied together by a red bow. "Serena, this nice man has a couple of questions for you about Cindy. Okay?"

Serena nodded.

I turned to her and asked, "Did you walk home with Cindy last Friday afternoon?"

"Yes," Serena said, nodding her head for emphasis.

"Did you go into the house with Cindy?"

"No, I stayed on the sidewalk and watched her run into the house."

My forehead wrinkled and I paused for a moment. "Run? Why would Cindy *run* to the house?"

Serena shrugged her shoulders. "I don't know. I guess she was happy because someone was home."

"Hold on. Did you see someone in the house?"

"Sort of," Serena said, tilting her head. "I saw someone downstairs through the window."

I sat up in my chair. "You don't know who it was?" I asked.

Serena shook her head before saying, "It's pretty far from the sidewalk to the house. And my eyes aren't that great."

"She's right," Serena's mother chimed in. "We've been delaying getting her glasses for a while now."

"Can you describe this person in the house? Was the person male or female? Adult or child?"

"No, I can't. It was too far."

"Honey," Serena's mother said. "Why didn't you tell the police about the person in the house?"

"They didn't ask me about the person in the house," Serena responded innocently.

I had made major headway in this investigation. Someone who lived in the house had kidnapped Cindy. She wouldn't have excitedly run toward the house if she saw a stranger. But who did she see? Brian, Linda, Alice or Matthew? And where is Cindy now? Is she still alive? Unfortunately, I had a lot more questions than answers.

I drove back to my apartment, knowing, with each passing hour, the likelihood of ever finding Cindy Flowers was diminished. If I wanted to get to the truth quickly, I knew I needed help. Someone I could trust. I called Riley.

"I can't believe you're calling me," Riley said over the phone. "I just got chewed out by Metzger. I can't talk to you about this case."

"I just got a major lead in Cindy's disappearance and I need your help."

"Did you hear what I just said? I can't talk to you. My boss said..."

"Forget about Metzger. He can't control what you do in your personal time. All I'm asking you to do is to stop by my place when you get off work." I paused and noted a silence which meant Riley was unsure what to do. "Come on, Riley. I'm telling you I found out some information that might lead us to Cindy. Think about that darling ten year old. Who knows what someone could..."

"Alright, alright! I'll be by around six."

"Thanks."

After I hung up the phone, I decided to take a look at the videotape that Linda gave me. I looked at the first tape and I quickly fell in love with this charming, talented little girl.

The highlight of the tape was when Cindy was working on a magic act. Cindy was all dressed as a magician smiling from ear to ear. She was so cute. She made a deck of cards and a stuffed bunny rabbit disappear. I sat back in my chair and wondered who was the magician who made *Cindy* disappear.

As soon as that tape ended, I quickly grabbed the other videotape. It told a completely different story. Based on the date displayed on the bottom of the screen, the video was taken about five and a half months ago.

Cindy was singing, but what immediately caught my attention was that she had her right arm in a sling. She was singing relatively well, but she would forget the words to the song. Brian's voice soon followed saying, "Come on Cindy. You'll never become a Miss Junior America if you can't remember the words."

Cindy shot back, "I'm tired and my arm hurts. I don't want to sing any more."

Cindy walked out of the view of the camera and Brian grabbed her left arm and pulled her back. "You will continue to practice this until you sing it right, young lady."

"I want mommy! I miss her. Where is she?"

"Your mommy's not here! You have a talent and I'm not letting it go to waste. You're going to be a star."

"I don't want to be a star!" Cindy said amidst tears.

"Yes, you do," Brian said as he grabbed and shook her. I looked on in shock, seeing Brian as some kind of monster. As I watched, I kept wondering. Where was Linda? And how did Cindy's arm get in a sling?

My doorbell rang. I shut the television off and walked to the door.

"Okay, what's the big lead you have?" Riley asked, walking into my house.

"Have a seat on the couch," I said, closing the door. "I'll tell you in a minute, but watch this first." I turned on the television and push play on the VCR. I let the tape go for about twenty seconds, looking at Riley the whole time. I pushed pause on the tape and stared at Riley. "Well, can you explain that?"

"Brian Flowers is a tyrannical father, living vicariously through his daughter," Riley said with no emotion. "But, I knew that already."

"How about Cindy's arm?" I asked, pointing. "How did it get in a sling?"

Riley's forehead wrinkled as he leaned forward toward the television. "I don't know. I wasn't aware Cindy had an accident."

"Maybe it was no accident."

"You're really speculating."

"I don't know. I saw him violently shake her on videotape."

"I told you that Brian hit his wife. I already knew he was a violent man. Now, please tell me that wasn't the reason you wanted me to come here."

"No, it's not," I said, turning the television off. "I want you to do background checks on all four people who live in that house. I have reason to believe that one of the four kidnapped Cindy."

"What basis?" Riley asked with a serious look on his face.

"I talked to Serena, the girl who walked home with Cindy Friday afternoon. She said she saw someone in the house downstairs and she also saw Cindy happily run up to the house."

"Stop right there," Riley said, holding his right hand up. "I checked with everyone who lived there. No one was home at that time."

"One of them is lying," I said bluntly.

"Maybe little ten year old Serena is mistaken. And she didn't mention any of this to me when I spoke to her." Riley paused a moment before saying, "If Serena saw someone in the window, why all the mystery? Why can't she say which family member she saw?"

"She wasn't able to identify anyone. Her eye sight isn't too good from far away."

Riley groaned and ran his hands through his hair on the top of his head. "You're relying on something a ten year old girl with bad eye sight says she sees."

"Just think about it for a moment. Serena's eye sight may be poor, but it was good enough to see someone. And Cindy can corroborate Serena's eye sight."

"Cindy? What are you talking about?"

"Serena said Cindy ran to the house excited because someone was home. With her perfect eyesight, Cindy must have seen someone too. Someone she was excited about seeing. Someone she knew."

"You don't know that for sure. It could have been a stranger who broke in the house."

"Well, for starters what kind of evidence showed the house was broken into?"

"None, but that doesn't mean that…"

"What things did the Flowers tell you were stolen from the house?"

"Nothing, but the kidnapper may have only been interested in taking Cindy."

"Okay, tell me which neighbors heard loud barking that afternoon?"

"Barking?" Riley asked, confused.

"Yeah barking. Alice's dog was home at that time. And believe me that dog would bark like crazy if any stranger got near that house."

Riley paused a moment to sigh deeply. "I'll run that background check for you tonight."

While Riley was running the background checks, I set out to check the alibi that each of the four offered for Friday afternoon. But, of the four, only Matthew would appear to have an alibi that could easily be corroborated. He said he was at basketball practice when Cindy disappeared.

I raced over to watch Mathew's junior varsity basketball game at seven o'clock. The school gym was packed on this Sunday night. Throughout the game, I kept looking for either Alice, Brian, or Linda. I never saw any of them. I did see Matthew. He never moved from his position on the bench. I was shocked. I had gotten the impression that he was a star player.

After the game, I jumped out of the stands and rushed over to Matthew. Before I could say anything, he told me to "get lost".

I jogged over to his coach. "I'm a friend of Matthew Flowers. Why didn't he play?"

The coach's answer was succinct. "Everyone on the team knows my policy. If you miss a practice, you sit on the bench for the next game."

"Matthew missed a practice? Which one?"

"Friday," the coach answered as he walked away. It was a shocking way to end my first day on the case.

I awoke to a very cold Monday morning, even though the sun was out. I turned on the radio and they warned there would likely be a snowstorm tonight. I got a frantic call from Brian, telling me to come down to the police station immediately. When I got to the police station, I saw Brian and Linda talking to Sheriff Metzger in his office. Even though the door was closed, I could hear Brian yelling, "I can't believe this! Why aren't you doing anything?"

Riley was at his desk just outside Metzger's office. He got up and walked over to me. "I suppose you heard the news."

"No. What's going on?"

"Matthew has disappeared." My heart sank and I quickly passed Riley and opened the door of the sheriff's office.

"What are you doing here?" Sheriff Metzger asked as he rose from his chair. "I thought I told you that..."

"I called him down here sheriff," Brian said. "I want him to be here."

Sheriff Metzger grumbled to himself as he sat back down.

I closed the door. "What happened?"

"The kidnapper has struck again," Linda said, wiping off a tear. "First, Cindy was taken. Now, Matthew."

"And the police aren't doing anything about it!" Brian shouted, gesturing toward Sheriff Metzger.

"As I said before, according to the law, a teenager is not considered missing until 24 hours. And you said that you saw him before he went off to his basketball game last night."

"I was at that game," I said, which caused surprised looks by everyone in the room. "He was there the whole game. His team lost."

"See that," Sheriff Metzger said, pointing to me. "He probably just stayed at a friend's house last night to mourn the loss."

"We already told you that we checked with all his friends and none of them know where he is," Linda said. "And he didn't show up to school this morning."

"You waited to start looking for Cindy," Brian said. "Don't make the same mistake again."

"We're working on some strong leads in the Cindy Flowers investigation," Sheriff Metzger said.

"Like what?" I asked.

"I can't say right now," Sheriff Metzger said, glaring at me. It was one thing to have to answer to the grief stricken parents of a missing child. But, he wasn't about to take it from me. Metzger added, "As soon as I have anything solid, I'll let the *family* know."

Linda and Brian left the police station in a state of desperation, frustration, and anger. Before Sheriff Metzger could throw me out of the police station, Riley told me to come back at six o'clock, when Metzger's shift would be over. In the meantime, I decided to visit the community center where Alice spent her afternoons. I found Alice inside playing bridge. I noted the large number of senior citizens and activities at the community center. It was conceivable that Alice could leave without being missed.

"What are you doing here?" Alice said as I approached the table.

"My job, and I just found out I have to find Matthew as well as Cindy."

"Well, they're not here," Alice said. "I checked."

I noticed my presence had brought the bridge game to a halt. I asked Alice for a moment of her time. She reluctantly agreed. Alice grabbed her cane and we slowly walked over to a corner in the large game room. "I wanted to ask you a question," I said. "While Linda and Brian have spent every waking hour looking for Cindy, it doesn't appear her or Matthew's disappearance has changed your routine at all. Am I right? Have you been looking?"

"I've been praying. It's in God's hands now." Alice closed her eyes before repeating, "Yes, God will bring Cindy home soon." Alice quickly made the sign of the cross.

"What about Matthew?" I asked with raised eyebrows. "You don't seem too concerned about him."

"Oh yes, of course. God will bring him home too." She turned and walked back toward the card table.

It was six o'clock on a cold Monday evening when I made it back to the police station. As soon as I arrived, Riley raced to the front to meet me. "Metzger is still here."

I glanced at Metzger's office and could see him working on his computer. "What's he doing here so late?"

"He said he had a hot lead in the Flowers case. He won't tell me what it is."

"Has Matthew turned up yet?"

"No," Riley said, looking at his watch. "It's almost 24 hours since you saw him. He'll be officially missing soon."

"Well, well, well, look what we have here," Sheriff Metzger said, strutting out of his office. His chest stuck out like a proud peacock and he looked as pompous and arrogant as ever. "With the help of another office," he said, waving a sheet of paper. "I just found Cindy Flowers."

I was stunned. Riley appeared equally floored. After Sheriff Metzger folded the sheet of paper and put it in his shirt pocket, I asked on impulse. "Where did you find her? Is she alive?"

"I believe that qualifies as none of your business," Sheriff Metzger said. "Now, get out of here."

I knew it was no use arguing with him. I turned around and headed out of the police station. I decided that I needed to clear my head tonight and forget about this case. Sheriff Metzger apparently had already found Cindy and I doubt Linda and Brad would continue to pay me to locate Matthew. I was relaxing on my reclining chairs as I channel surfed. I stopped when I saw Linda Flowers. She was on a local, independent station telling how her two children were missing. They flashed Cindy and Matthew's picture on the screen. At that moment, my phone rang causing me to instinctively look at the clock. It was 8:15. I muted the television and picked up the phone.

"Robert, it's Riley. I need your help."

"What's wrong?"

"You need to come to the Flowers estate as soon as possible. Metzger was murdered on the front door step of the Flowers estate."

"Oh no," I said in a state of shock. I mumbled, "I'll be there in ten minutes."

When I arrived at the Flowers' estate on this brisk, cold night, snow began to rain down from the sky, stronger than the light snow flurries of yesterday. The elements were starting to make things more challenging for the team of police officers and plain-clothes forensic experts in front of the house. Riley emerged from the sea of investigators and walked over to me.

"What happened?" I asked, holding both arms out. I could see my breath as I talked.

"Someone bashed his head in on the front doorstep," Riley said, pointing to the awning covered front porch. As he talked, Riley used his gloved right hand to shield his face from the falling snow.

"Front of his head or back?"

"Toward the back," Riley responded.

I looked at my watch. "We both saw him about two and a half hours ago. What did he do after I left?"

"He left shortly after you did. Maybe ten, fifteen minutes top. He was coming here to tell them that he had found Cindy Flowers."

"What *exactly* was he going to tell the Flowers? Was he going to tell them Cindy was alive or dead?"

"I don't know," Riley said, shrugging his shoulders. "He didn't tell me anything about his big discovery."

"He didn't tell his most senior deputy?"

"No. He just kept saying that I'd probably tell you and you'd try to take credit." I rubbed my cold forehead with my right hand in frustration and let out a small groan. Riley continued, "I was on patrol when I got the call from the dispatcher to get over here. As senior deputy, I'm acting sheriff now. I've sealed the crime scene. The coroner took the body. Forensics are doing their job."

"Well, you better hurry. I heard on the radio the snowstorm is only going to get worse."

"Yep, that's what I heard," Riley said. "Hey, it's freezing out here. Let's go inside."

As we entered the front door, I could see the outline of where Metzger's body was found on the porch. His head was closer to the door with his feet pointing out toward the street. We walked into the family room. Brian and Alice were sitting in the living room waiting for Riley. Brian had a beer in his hand and Alice was rubbing her dog who sat on her lap. "What are you doing here?" Brian asked as I entered the room.

"Robert saw the victim about six o'clock," Riley responded before I could say anything. "He's here because I have some questions for him. I thought it would be easier to question all of you at once. Brian, let's start with you since you discovered the body."

"I got an anonymous phone call around six thirty from someone who said they had Cindy," Brian said. "The person says to bring two thousand in cash to Buckley Liquors by seven o'clock if I ever want to see Cindy alive. So, I go by my bank and head to the liquor store."

"Why didn't you notify the police?" Riley asked.

"Because the caller said they'd kill Cindy if I told anyone. Anyway, no one was there. I waited for about thirty minutes. By 7:30, I figured it was a hoax and came home. When I got home, I parked in the driveway and when I get to the front door, I see the sheriff lying dead on my doorstep with his head bashed in."

"What time did you get home?" Riley asked.

"I don't know. I guess 7:45."

"How about you Alice?" Riley asked. "How did you spend your evening?"

"I know you're trying to figure out who killed that sheriff," Alice said. "It wasn't Brian or me. I believe it was an act of God. Vengeance is mine sayeth the Lord."

Riley sighed heavily and rested his forehead on his left hand before saying, "Alice, all I want to know is how you spent your evening."

Alice looked back at Riley with disdain as she grabbed her cane with her left hand while continuing to gently rub her dog with the right. "I got back from the community center about five o'clock. When I got home, I chatted with Brian until the phone rang. It was about six thirty. Brian went to get the phone and I went upstairs to my room to take a nap."

"Did you actually go to sleep?"

"Why yes," Alice replied as she tightened her grip on her cane. "A long nap too. Didn't wake up until eight o'clock. That's when Brian came to my room to tell me about the sheriff. I'm telling you that God took that sheriff's life, for not trying to find Cindy."

I left the crime scene that night depressed. As much as I was sickened by Sheriff Metzger's murder, I was more heartbroken by its timing. Metzger was going to tell the family that he found her. In the best case scenario, Cindy would be back home alive if Metzger wasn't murdered. In the worst case scenario, the Flowers family would at least have some much-needed closure.

His death at the Flowers' doorstep had to be somehow connected with Cindy's disappearance. But how? Perhaps Metzger told the kidnapper about his discovery and the kidnapper killed him to keep Cindy's whereabouts a secret.

I tossed and turned in my sleep as I tried to figure things out. No answers were coming to me. Just more questions, like what ever happened to Matthew Flowers?

I finally gave up the task of sleeping at about seven in the morning. When I got out of bed, I noticed a blanket of snow outside. It had stopped snowing now. Looking at the pristine Winter wonderland as I drank my coffee, I thought about Cindy. It was Tuesday morning, about 89 hours since she disappeared. As I counted the hours, I knew that time was the enemy. I hoped she was alive. I hoped she was safe.

I was eating a late breakfast when my doorbell rang. I walked down the hallway and opened my front door.

"Less than a day as sheriff, and I found one of the children," Riley said, letting himself into my house. Cold air rushed in from outside and I quickly closed the door.

"You found Cindy?"

"No, Matthew. Picked him up at a breakfast joint on a tip from the store manager. I took him back to his parents. Turns out no one kidnapped him. He just ran away from home."

"Great work," I said.

"Yeah, well, there's a new sheriff in town."

I chuckled as we both took a seat in the living room. "You know, everyone was so concerned about Cindy's disappearance. I bet he just did it for the attention."

Riley nodded his head. "I came by because I never did get back to you on those background checks." I smiled, pleased that Riley didn't forget. "Matthew has a rap sheet a mile long, shoplifting, trespassing, disturbing the peace."

"Sounds like a boy scout."

"Well, let's just say he's a chip off the ole block," Riley said. "His father Brian assaulted a police officer once. He has also been charged with destruction of property. He put his hand through someone's car window because he said they gave him the finger. And like I told you before, I know he beat his wife. I saw the bruises with my own eyes."

"How about the women of the household?"

"Alice and Linda's records are completely clean."

I scratched my head. "Did you question Linda about her whereabouts last night around the time Metzger was murdered?"

"Yeah. She's got an alibi. She was doing a live interview at the television station that ran from eight until nine o'clock. But, I have witnesses that can vouch that she was there for an hour and a half before the program preparing."

"What about Matthew? Does he have an alibi for last night?"

"He says that he was hiding out in his friend's garage all night. He claimed that his friend can vouch for him. But, when I questioned his friend, he admitted he wasn't with Matthew all the time, like when his friend went inside to have dinner with his family."

"Do you know when that was?" I asked.

"The friend says around seven."

"I remember Metzger waving a sheet of paper in his hand and putting it in his shirt pocket. It seemed to be some kind of information about Cindy's disappearance."

"I know what you're talking about," Riley said, nodding his head. "I remember that too. I asked Metzger if I could see it after you left, but he wouldn't show me."

"My question is whether you found the sheet of paper on Metzger's dead body?"

Riley shook his head as he paused to think. "I hadn't thought of that, but no. Wasn't on him." Riley scratched his head. "Metzger was missing something else too."

"What?"

"His billy club."

"Could he just have taken it off?"

"No, it's standard procedure to always wear a billy club. He always wore it."

"So why would the killer take his billy club?" I asked. Riley paused a moment before responding by shrugging his shoulders.

A ton of things flashed through my mind. What happened to that sheet of paper? Did Metzger take it to the Flowers estate that night? If not, what did he do with it? If so, why wasn't it on his dead body? Did his killer take it? If so, how did they even know about it? Did Metzger show it to his killer? And what happened to his billy club? Could it have been the murder weapon? But if so, how did the killer get it off such a strong, trained man like Sheriff Metzger.

"Want to know what I think?" Riley asked, breaking my concentration.

"Yes, of course."

"I think the person who killed Metzger also kidnapped that little girl. The killer was trying to cover up the kidnapping. And with Cindy's friend's testimony, that means it had to be either Brian, Linda, Matthew, or Alice."

"But, Linda has an alibi," I said.

"That's right. I talked to the coroner. The blow to Metzger's head would have had to take a great amount of strength. I don't think Alice could have pulled it off."

"Don't be too sure. Looks can sometimes be deceiving."

"Well, I don't think so," Riley retorted. "So, that just leaves me with Brian and Matthew. I think it was Brian."

"Why?"

"Because of that phony alibi that he gave about the ransom call. He said the kidnappers asked for $2,000. Now, think about it. No kidnapper would ask for that little. Brian must have made it up."

Riley's transistor radio began making noises as I pondered Riley's last point. "Riley, this is Deputy Petersen, are you out there?"

Riley pulled out his transistor radio. "This is Riley. What's up Petersen?"

"We got the search warrant."

"Great!" Riley said with a thump on the table. "Get over to Flowers house on the double. I'm leaving now."

As Riley got up, I grabbed his arm. "I want you to be careful. Someone in that house is a killer. Remember what happened to Metzger."

"I'll be careful," Riley said as he headed out the door.

"I want to come. I think I should come."

Riley paused for a moment as if to think it over. "Sure, come on."

I followed Riley's squad car to the Flowers' house. With snow covering the roads, we drove at a more deliberate pace. Barren trees that lined the road were blanketed with snow. Deputy Petersen was waiting for us on the street in front of the house and handed Riley the search warrant. Petersen was a young, clean-shaven officer with short black hair. In his mid twenties, I'd guess that the handsome deputy was quite the heartthrob among young ladies in the town. Petersen appeared respectful of Riley, acutely aware of the chain of command. When the three of us arrived at the front door and rang the doorbell, loud yapping noises were heard, followed by Alice's voice saying, "Shush Spider, shush!"

Alice let us in and, with cane in hand, slowly led us into the family room. As we all sat down in the family room, Brian entered the room saying, "I hope you're here to tell me you found Cindy."

"Unfortunately, we're not," Riley said. "But, I need to see everyone now. Please get Linda and Matthew." I knew Riley wanted to inform the whole family at the same time of the search warrant and ask that they all leave immediately.

"Linda! Come into the living room!" Brian shouted before taking a seat next to Alice. As Linda entered the room, Brian said, "Matthew is not feeling well. You're going to have to talk to him later."

Riley paused for a moment as he eyed both Linda and Brian. "I don't care how he feels, I want him down here. I have something I have to tell all of you."

"In that case," Brian said rising. "I'll go get him." Brian returned a couple of minutes later with Matthew. Wearing long pants and long sleeve shirt, Matthew sported several bruises on his face.

"What happened to you?" Riley asked as the two entered the room.

"I fell from a tree in the backyard."

Riley walked up to Matthew. "You're telling me a fall from a tree did this to your face." Matthew nodded. Riley turned toward Brian. "Is this true? He fell from a tree?"

"That's what the boy said."

Riley paused a moment before saying, "You're under arrest."

"For what?" Brian asked, putting his hands on his hips.

Riley stood frozen, apparently paralyzed in a combination of anger, frustration, and confusion. He glanced at me before looking back at Brian. "I'm arresting you for the murder of Sheriff Larry Metzger and the..."

"You're what?" Brian said in shock.

"Riley, no," I said approaching him.

"Stay out of this!" Riley said to me. He then focused back on Brian. "I'm arresting you for the murder of Larry Metzger and the kidnapping of Cindy Flowers."

"You're accusing me of kidnapping my own dau..."

"Petersen, read him his rights," Riley said.

As the deputy read him his rights, Brian wasn't listening. He was too busy making threats, promising Riley that he'd "never work as a police officer ever again" and that he'd "sue the whole town".

While Riley led the search effort at the house, Deputy Petersen took a handcuffed Brian to the police station. I followed the squad car to the station. It began snowing again. New snow fell on the already snow-covered road. After Brian was booked, I had a short opportunity to talk to him.

Brian told me to stop looking for Cindy and to focus 100% of my efforts on clearing his name. He said he would pay a $100,000 bonus if I could prove that he was innocent. I remained silent with my mouth wide open, stunned by the sum. In my twenty years as a private investigator, I had never been offered anything near that amount. He said that he'd have his lawyers draw up a contract by the end of the day.

Petersen interrupted us to take Brian to a holding cell. He promised that I could meet with Brian later. While I was waiting, I saw Riley return to the station and enter his new office. I raced over to talk to him.

"You're arresting Brian for the wrong reason," I said, just as he took a seat at his desk. "You're arresting him because you know he's a wife beater and a child abuser. But that doesn't make him a murderer."

Riley looked at me for a moment as he thought about his response. "He deserves to be behind bars."

"Not for murder. You have no direct evidence that Brian murdered Sheriff Metzger."

"Brian was the only one strong enough to do it. Metzger was a big man."

"Oh come on, you said Metzger's wound was at the back of his head," I said, gesturing toward the back of my head. "So the murderer hit him from behind. Surprised him. Matthew and Linda are both strong enough to do it. Maybe Alice too."

"Linda has an alibi." Riley took his glasses off and rubbed the bridge of his nose, apparently mentally exhausted. "Look, I have appreciated your help. I really have. But, I think it's just best that you leave," Riley said rising.

"Sorry, I can't leave," I said also rising. "I'm here to see Brian. I talked to him for a few minutes earlier. Petersen promised me a longer visit." Riley stood frozen in complete shock. His face contorted. He appeared to be displeased, possibly even feeling betrayed.

"Brian hired you to find Cindy," Riley said, looking at me with a slight head tilt. "Cindy's not with Brian. So why do you have to see him?"

"I'm not looking for Cindy right now. I'm working for Brian to prove his innocence."

"Prove his innocence? He's not innocent. He beats his wife and son. He's a menace." Riley squinted as if to indicate that he was having trouble recognizing me. "I'm disappointed, very disappointed."

Riley led me back to Brian's cell. He didn't say anything to me on our short journey. He opened the cell door and immediately closed it after I walked in. The cell bars made a loud clanging sound as the cell door locked. It was an awful sound, the sound of lost freedom. I felt claustrophobic in the small cell. The only furniture was a thin bed attached to the wall. "You have ten minutes," Riley said before leaving us.

I looked over to Brian who was in a lousy mood and appeared to be waiting until Riley was out of earshot to erupt. Brian got up from his bed and said, "Riley will pay for this. The whole town will pay." Then, Brian began cursing Linda's name as he paced back and forth in his cell like a caged lion. "She said she wants a divorce. I can't believe she's deserting me when I…"

"Hey!" Brian stood motionless, shocked that I had raised my voice. "You're going to have to focus if I'm going to be able to help you."

Brian slowly took a seat next to me on the bed in the cell. He rested his elbows on his knees and his chin on his clasped hands. "I have a team of lawyers helping me with the legal maneuvering. But, I don't want this thing to ever go to trial. I can't afford the hit to my public persona." Brian pointed to me. "If you prove my innocence and stop this from ever going to trial, you can save my reputation. You can save my marriage. You can save my life."

"You'll have to be completely honest with me."

"Of course," Brian said nodding.

"Did you hit Matthew earlier today?"

"What does that have to do with getting me out of here?"

"I need to understand your relationship with your family. It's entirely possible one of them killed Metzger." There was a pause as I let Brian think about what I just said. "Did you hit Matthew?" I asked again.

"Yeah, I hit him."

"Why?"

"Because of that stunt he pulled. Running away, worrying Linda and me. Distracting us from finding Cindy."

"Was that the first time you ever hit him?"

Brian shook his head. "I'm not proud of that," he said, looking down at the ground.

"What about Cindy? Have you ever hit her?" Brian took a deep breath before nodding his head. My heart sank. "You hit Cindy. How could you do that?"

"I just snapped. It was a momentary lapse. This is no excuse, but Linda has done far worse."

"What did Linda do?"

"She was drunk driving and got into an accident, injuring Cindy's arm."

"When was this?"

"About six months ago?"

"That was about when you wanted me to spy on Linda?"

"Yeah, I wanted leverage against my wife. She threatened to divorce me and take Cindy away. She changed her mind after the accident."

"Time's up," Riley said, unlocking the cell. I said a quick goodbye to Brian and headed out of the cell. Riley insisted that I come into his office. We sat down and he said, "I thought you might want to know you're working for a murderer. I just got a call from..."

"What is it with you? Why do you have it in for this guy? Because he's a wife beater? A child abuser?"

Riley simply stared back for a moment. "I have it in for this guy because he murdered a police officer and a friend."

"Do you know something that I don't know?"

"Yeah, I do. Remember Metzger's missing billy club." I nodded my head as Riley continued, "During the search of the house, it was found underneath Brian's mattress. The lab just called and notified me that the club has small traces of blood on it. AB Positive. That was Metzger's blood type and it's rare." I slumped in my chair. "It gets worse. The lab identified a strand of hair found on Metzger's dead body that belongs to Brian Flowers."

I paused for a moment. "Where was the hair found on his body?"

"On Metzger's back. The forensics team found it."

"Were there any fingerprints on the club?"

"None."

"Not even Metzger's?"

"No," Riley said, shaking his head. "When Brian wiped his off, he must have taken Metzger's away too." Riley got up from his chair and walked around his desk before sitting down on the front edge of his desk facing me. "This is what I think happened. Our boy scout back there, who beats his wife and son, snaps one day and hits little Cindy. He injures her badly or maybe even kills her. He panics and gets rid of the body. Metzger finds this out and goes over to the house to arrest him." I looked at Riley. Part of me was proud of him. His reasoning seemed to make sense so far. He adjusted his glasses and continued, "Brian probably distracts Metzger, takes his billy club away, and clocks him. While he's leaning over to check the body for any evidence, a strand of hair falls onto the body. Later, he hides the club under his bed." Riley slid off the desk and walked back to his chair.

"Do you think it's possible that the murderer planted Brian's hair on the body and Metzger's billy club under Brian's mattress?"

Riley clasped both hands on top of his head in frustration as he leaned back in his chair. "How much is Brian paying you to get him out of here? If he paid $20,000 to find his daughter, I bet he'd pay even more to save his own hide."

I thought about refusing to answer the question. But, I knew that would just serve to antagonize Riley and show that I was embarrassed. "$100,000. I know it seems high, but he's paying for my investigatory skills and my history on this case."

"I tell you about conclusive physical evidence against Brian and the first thing you can say is that he was framed. I think that he bought much more than your investigatory skills. He bought you."

Sometimes the worst punishment is when a friend holds up a mirror. And when that friend is Riley, a consistently moral and law upholding man, it hurts that much more. Had Brian bought me? Was I letting my potential financial gain cloud my judgment? Was I being employed by a kidnapping murderer? Or was my gut instinct right? That someone was trying to frame Brian Flowers. But if someone was trying to frame him, who? Who could have gotten a strand of his hair and who could have planted that billy club under his mattress?

"If Brian was the kidnapper, why would he hire me and then offer these large bonuses?"

Riley grabbed a nearby tissue. He took off his eye-glasses and began wiping them with the tissue. As he did this, he asked, "How much would you be willing to offer me if I could run 40 mph.?"

"As much money as you want because it's impossible."

"Exactly," Riley said, putting his glasses back on. "Brian offered you $20,000 to find Cindy alive because he knew he killed her. Then, he offered you $100,000 to prove he's innocent because he knows he's guilty." I rubbed my chin thinking about Riley's last comment and wondering whether there was any merit to it. "The reason I'm telling you all this is that you have a pretty good reputation in this town. Your business depends on that. When it's proven in court that Brian Flowers is a child abuser and a murderer, it's not going to look good for you to be defending him. I recommend that you quit."

I got up from my chair slowly. "Thanks for your advice, but there's something more important than my image. It's justice. And I can't quit until I'm sure that justice is taking place."

I drove over to the Flowers' house to confront the person that I felt was responsible for Sheriff Metzger's death. It was 4:30 in the afternoon on Tuesday. It was over four full days since Cindy's disappearance. I rang the doorbell and immediately heard the yapping of Spider. My mind was wandering, thinking about where Spider was when Metzger came to the house the night he was murdered. Alice said she went to sleep. And she wasn't awakened until Brian came into her room to say that Metzger was dead. But when Metzger rang the doorbell that night, Spider should have been barking. And if Spider was barking, it should have awakened Alice. Why didn't it?

"Robert," Linda said, opening the front door. Spider seemed to recognize me and stopped barking once Linda invited me in. Linda escorted me into the dining room. I declined her offer for coffee and we sat down at the dining room table. The long table, which was well lit by the hanging chandelier, seemed awkwardly large for two people.

"So are you any closer to finding my little girl?" Linda asked with her hands clasped together.

I shook my head, which caused Linda to sigh. "Brian told me you've filed for a divorce. Why?"

"Let's just say irreconcilable differences and leave it at that."

"I didn't mean to pry," I said, trying to be polite. "I was looking at those videotapes that you gave me. I saw Cindy's arm was in a sling. Now how did that happen?"

Linda paused for about five seconds looking off in the distance. "She hurt it in a car accident," Linda said, looking back at me.

I nodded my head. I slowly rose from my chair. I hadn't come to talk to Linda. This was a good time to ask about the person I came to see, the person I suspected killed Metzger. "Is Matthew around?"

Linda escorted me upstairs and knocked on Matthew's closed door. Matthew yelled to come in. There was clear disappointment shown on his face as I entered. Linda left us alone, closing the door after she left. As I pulled a chair away from his desk, I looked at Matthew who was resting on his unmade bed. I placed the chair near the head of the bed and sat down. Noticing Matthew's bruises on his face, I felt sick to my stomach knowing that the man I was working for had done this to his son. I kept telling myself that I had to be concerned with what the young boy had done to his sister.

"Where were you last Friday afternoon? The time when Cindy was abducted."

"I already told you," Matthew said as he got up and walked over to his desk, probably to get away from me. "I was at basketball practice."

"No, you weren't. I talked to your coach. He says you missed Friday's practice. That's why you didn't play in the next game. Why did you lie?"

"You know, I don't have to answer your questions."

"I think you lied because you were really waiting at your house to kidnap your sister."

"You're crazy."

"But, you didn't stop there," I said, looking directly at Matthew. "You disappeared for a few days, hiding out at a friend's house. When he went inside to have dinner with his family, you snuck back home. That's when you encountered Sheriff Metzger. He told you that he suspected you of kidnapping Cindy and you killed him."

"Are you on drugs? I didn't kill nobody."

"You gave yourself away on the ransom money," I said, walking up to Matthew. "Only a kid would ask for only $2,000. An adult would have asked for much more. You were trying to extort money from your father with that call."

"Get out of here," Matthew said, gesturing toward the door.

"Metzger figured all this out. So when he came over, you grabbed away his billy club and hit him hard in back of the head." I said now in Matthew's face, "You grabbed his billy club and you hit him in the back of the..." I stopped in mid sentence. It hit me like a shot. The smaller Matthew couldn't have murdered Metzger, not the way he died.

Matthew, at first stunned by the abrupt silence, said, "I want you to leave, now."

I slowly walked out of Matthew's room and headed for my car. I was confused, in a daze, wondering. Trying to answer one very large question. How did Metzger's killer get his billy club away and then use it to bash him over the head? The back of the head, as if he was fleeing. He'd never flee when he was trained for over fifteen years to be aggressive and in control. He would have drawn his gun. So how did the killer succeed?

When I returned to the police station, it was five o'clock. I expected Riley might be packing to leave for the day. But as I looked into his office, it appeared he was doing packing of a more permanent variety. Stacks of cardboard boxes were just outside his office.

"What are you doing?"

"I'm going on administrative leave," Riley said as he continued to put things in boxes. "They're bringing in a sheriff tomorrow. Metzger died last night and they have already assigned his permanent replacement. Pretty quick, huh?"

"You can't leave now. What about Cindy? You're just going to give up?" One trait Riley showed over the last nine years is his ability to persevere.

"You can call it what if you want. I need some time away." Riley continued to pack and I just watched him for a few moments, feeling very uncomfortable. "Petersen is in the back. He can help you." Riley held out his hand. He gave me his traditionally firm handshake, as he looked me right in the eye. "I'll call you in a few weeks once I have a chance to unwind. Maybe we can go fishing."

"I'd like that," I said before turning to leave.

I found Petersen and he led me back to talk to Brian. I needed to give Brian some good news. So, I used the same argument I used to clear Matthew as a suspect in Metzger's murder and applied it to Brian. I told him it was unreasonable to believe Metzger would flee if you grabbed his billy club. And since Metzger was hit in the back of the head, he had to be fleeing.

Over the next couple of weeks, this case continued to befuddle me. Because of what Serena told me the first day I was on the job, I still believed that someone in the household kidnapped Cindy. And I thought the kidnapping and Metzger's murder on the Flowers' estate were connected, especially considering Metzger had just found Cindy. But, how could anyone in that house, even Brian, take Metzger's billy club away and then bash him on the back of the head before Metzger could even reach for his gun. It just didn't make sense.

The new sheriff decided that there was enough evidence to uphold Brian's arrest and the town d.a. agreed to prosecute Brian for second degree murder. Brian responded by hiring a team of high priced lawyers that he felt confident would prove his innocence, or at least reasonable doubt. Brian had no trouble posting the large bail so that he could be a free man until the trial.

As happy as Brian was to be out of jail, it was greatly mitigated by the fact that Linda had formally filed the divorce papers and left town. Every time I saw Brian he insisted his lawyers, with the aid of a prenuptial agreement, would make sure Linda would get very little of *his* large fortune. Alice supported her son strongly, saying that she "never thought Linda was good enough for him anyway". I barely saw Matthew. He went out of his way to avoid me after I accused him of killing Metzger.

I decided to stop by the police station late in the day.

Without Riley around, I didn't have any real friends left in the department. But I had gotten to know Deputy Petersen, a young officer who had seen me work with Riley over the last two years.

As soon as I entered the police station, I saw Petersen. Most of the other officers were either out in the field or off work so the office was pretty barren. "So, have you guys gotten any leads on Cindy Flowers?"

"I hate to say it, but it's been over two weeks. She's probably dead. No one around here is very optimistic anymore."

"But, you guys are sure about Brian being the murderer."

"That's the company line," Petersen said with smile.

"Go with me for a minute," I said before asking him to rise. I walked around his desk toward him. "If you were coming to arrest me at my house and I reached for your billy club like this," I said, stretching my hand out. "What would you do?"

Within half a second, Petersen drew his gun and pressed it against my head ordering me to "freeze!"

My heart beat rapidly as I felt a gun against my head. I swallowed hard before Petersen slowly removed the gun from my head and sat back down. "Now, why didn't Sheriff Metzger do that to his killer?"

"You mean to Brian. Maybe Brian distracted him somehow."

"Distracted him? Metzger came over there to make an arrest. How could Brian distract him? Wouldn't Metzger take every precaution possible?"

"Maybe not," Petersen said. "He should have brought backup to make an arrest, especially for a suspect as big as Brian Flowers. But, Metzger was an arrogant guy. He didn't always do things by the book. He just did things his way. You know, he..." Petersen stopped in mid sentence and waved his left hand in front of me in an attempt to stop me from daydreaming. "Are you listening to me?"

"Oh yeah, I am," I said slowly. "Because I listened to you, I now know who killed Metzger. The problem is I don't know why." Petersen looked at me bewildered, afraid to ask any questions for fear of a crazy answer. So, I beat him to a question. "Did you know Linda Flowers had a drunk driving arrest?"

"Of course, happened, uh, about six, seven months ago."

"You knew? How did you know?"

"Everyone on the police force knew. It was a pretty big deal. Cindy hurt her arm in the car crash. The Flowers are a pretty influential family in this town. So, Linda never faced prosecution."

"Why isn't Brian so lucky?"

"Drunk driving is not murder," Petersen said seriously. He leaned closer to me and said, "Word around town was that Linda was ready to divorce Brian. But after the accident, Linda reconsidered. If you ask me, I think she did so because Brian pulled some strings for her so she wouldn't stand trial and no one outside the police department would ever find out. I think she felt she owed him."

"Can I use the phone?"

"Be my guest," Petersen said, pointing to a nearby phone.

I hadn't talked to Brian yet today and I wanted to give an update.

"I'm getting tired of all this talk," Brian said over the phone. "I'm paying you for results and I'm seeing very little. What have you found out new that's going to keep me out of the courtroom?"

"Nothing yet, but I have a strong hunch…"

"Hunch? I'm not paying you for hunches." He sighed deeply. "You've been a big disappointment. Effective immediately, you're fired. Send me your final bill."

"Fired? Can you give me just two more days?" The only response was a dial tone. Brian had hung up on me. Still in shock, I looked over at Petersen.

"You don't look so good. What happened?"

I sat up in the chair. "Brian fired me."

"If you ask me, you're better off," Petersen said. "He's going down."

"I just wish I could have found Cindy. That's what this was supposed to be about. Did any other office call here with any leads about Cindy's disappearance?"

"A couple offices have called, but nothing has ever come of it. I got a call from an office asking for the sheriff. The guy was calling to make sure that the information that he had wasn't a match to Cindy Flowers."

"What ever happened?"

"I don't know," Petersen said, shrugging his shoulders. "Riley took care of it."

"Hmmm." My brain began working quickly. I again doubted Brian was the murderer. But, this time it was different. This time, I wasn't working for that $100,000. My suspicions were coming from a clear, unbiased mind. "What office was that?"

"The Honolulu police department."

"Thanks," I said smiling. "You've been most helpful."

"I'm not sure what I did, but you're welcome," Petersen said with a chuckle. "So now that you're not working for Brian, what's next for you?"

"I've been working really hard lately," I said, rising. "I think I deserve a vacation. A Hawaiian vacation, perhaps."

The cool breeze from the Western Hawaiian wind nearly blew off my hat as I walked up to Riley Lawton's condo. I did some work on my computer to determine the location of all the property owned by Riley Lawton. It came as little surprise that the only property that arose was in Hawaii. As I knocked on the door, I felt a thousand emotions as I was about to confront a friend.

The door opened, revealing a smiling Riley, who apparently was recovering from great laughter. Riley's expression quickly changed as he appeared in shock at my presence. He quickly walked out onto the porch, closing the front door to the condo. "What are you doing here?"

"I wanted to tell you that I figured out who killed Sheriff Metzger."

"You came across the country to tell me this," Riley said as his forehead wrinkled.

I nodded my head and Riley tilted his head slightly waiting for some explanation. "I didn't come alone," I said, pointing to the Hawaiian police officer who was watching us from his patrol car. Riley's facial expression changed again as he folded his arms in front of his chest. "The most puzzling thing about Metzger's death is how someone could bash him over the head with his billy club. I mean, how could the killer get Metzger's billy club away from an armed police man and then hit him in the back of the head?"

"Maybe something distracted him. A noise, maybe. Metzger turns and looks. Brian grabs the billy club and boom."

"I don't think so," I said, shaking my head. "Petersen told me that it's normal operating procedure for two officers, not one, to make an arrest. Metzger didn't go to the Flowers' house alone. You came with him. As you were walking up to the house, you used your billy club to bash his head in."

Riley seemed stunned and remained speechless as he just stared at me. "If I killed Metzger, why would I ask your help on finding the killer?"

"Once you started to frame him, you knew that Brian would hire me. By getting me to help you first, you hoped my loyalty would be split." Riley shook his head. "You knew after you killed Metzger, you'd be acting sheriff for awhile. So, you'd be able to call for a search of the Flowers' house. During that search, you planted a billy club with Metzger's blood underneath Brian's bed to implicate Brian."

"That is a lie."

"Well, we know that Metzger was killed before he ever got to the door because Alice said she was taking a nap. A knock on the door or a ring of the doorbell would have made the family dog bark like crazy, which would have awakened Alice."

"Four words. I had no motive," Riley said. "Without motive, there's no case. Brian was the one with the motive because he kidnapped Cindy."

"Brian didn't kidnap Cindy. You did, along with Linda."

"Me and Linda? You're crazy."

"Yes, you and Linda. You two are romantically involved. When Brian hired me to spy on Linda six months ago, I think you were the man that was with Linda at the hotel room when I took that picture. I think Linda wanted a divorce, but she wouldn't get custody of Cindy. And you know why."

Riley rolled his eyes. "Why?"

"You know why. That's the point. You always knew why. It's because she broke Cindy's arm when Linda was drunk driving. You knew that. Petersen said everyone at the department knew. But, you told me her record was clean when you did that background check. You didn't want me to be suspicious of Linda." Riley just shook his head and I continued, "The point is that with Linda's criminal record and with Brian's financial background, Brian would win any custody suit. That's what this was all about. A custody battle. You and Linda kidnapped Cindy because that was the only way the three of you could be together."

"It's a nice story," Riley said. "You still have no hard evidence that I killed Metzger."

"I do," I said. "Only three people knew about the fax Metzger got from the Hawaiian office- Metzger, you, and me. So if anyone else would have killed them, they wouldn't have known to steal the fax that gave the description of a girl like Cindy spotted in Hawaii."

"I've heard enough. I want you off my property now."

I looked back at the patrol car. "The Hawaiian police officer has a search warrant. I suspect when we go inside we'll see Cindy and Linda. Now, don't you want to do this without the search? It'll be easier on the girl."

Riley dropped his head. "If what you say is right, Linda and I go to jail and Cindy goes back to her father, a child abuser. He has hit Cindy in the past and will do it again." There was a momentary silence as we just looked at each other. "You have to do right by Cindy. Just turn around and tell that officer that you were mistaken."

I closed my eyes in an attempt to gain strength. "I'd love to do that, but you and Linda went further than just kidnapping. You committed murder. On top of that, you tried to frame an innocent man for that murder. I can't walk away from this."

"I may have tried to frame a man who didn't commit murder. But, Brian Flowers is not an innocent man." Riley turned around and walked to the edge of the porch. He swung around and said, "Okay, I admit I killed Metzger. But, that's where it stops. I did all of this *alone*. You can take me down to the police station right now, but you can't come into the house."

"Because Cindy is in there?" Riley nodded as I sighed heavily. "The police will still look for Cindy. Eventually, they'll find her."

"Let them look. At least she'll be safe until that day happens. Now, take me to the police station."

I looked at Riley for a moment before I said, "Okay."

Riley nodded. "Now, I just have to go inside and get some things. Please, wait here." He went back into the house.

While I waited, I gave a thumbs-up sign to the officer. I walked along the porch to a window that was only partially covered by curtains. I looked inside and my heartbeat quickened as I watched the scene. Riley was hugging Linda and then a beautiful little girl who I knew only from pictures and videotapes was Cindy Flowers. Moments later, Riley came back alone and said, "Let's go."

I spent the rest of the day at the police station. It was a strange feeling. One might think that Riley would hate my guts for being the cause of an arrest which would likely assure the rest of his life behind bars. I think he made peace with me when I agreed to bring him into the station rather than immediately search his condo. The only mystery that remained was why such a moral man committed murder.

"Snowball effect," Riley said as we sat in a small room in the police department. I looked at Riley with a puzzled expression on my face. "Picture a small little snowball on top of a snow-covered hill. I promised to protect the small town at the bottom of the hill. Unexpectedly, the snowball begins to roll down the hill. As it rolls, it continues to get bigger and bigger so you have to resort to more and more drastic measures to stop it. You do those measures not only because of your promise, but because you know the town is innocent. The town must be protected. Even if I have to sacrifice myself."

I shook my head wishing the end could be better for Riley. "Why did you make the promise in the first place?"

"To stop Brian. He beat his wife. I come out to the house and try to get Linda to press charges. At first, she refuses to admit she was abused. After a few more times, she becomes strong enough to admit it. I promised her that I'd protect her and Cindy. I promised her. I had just about convinced her to leave Brian. But when she had the car accident where Cindy was injured, there was no way she would be able to divorce Brian and keep Cindy. Brian threatened he'd argue that she was an incompetent parent if Linda dared to divorce him. The snowball got bigger and bigger. I told her I'd protect her, no matter what. After all, I loved her."

As Riley talked, he looked right at me and seemed relieved to shed the burden that he was carrying. "So, I came up with the idea to fake Cindy's disappearance. Then, Linda would divorce Brian and leave town. Linda, Cindy, and I start our lives together in peace. But, Metzger found out that Cindy was alive. He figured out she was staying with Linda's mother in Hawaii. The night he went over to the Flowers' house, he was going to arrest Linda. She would have never gotten custody of her child. She'd be declared an unfit mother and thrown in jail. It would have been my fault. I wouldn't have protected her. So, I had to eliminate Metzger before he brought harm. It was the only way.

I had to do what it took to stop the snowball. Linda had no idea that I killed him." Riley took a deep breath and sighed before saying, "In life, you have to make choices."

The door opened and Linda appeared, holding little Cindy's hand. Riley's jaw dropped. "What are you doing here?" Riley asked.

"I'm turning myself in," Linda said. "I'm tired of running and I don't want to run without you. My parents have agreed to fight for custody. But, I'm ready to face any punishment for kidnapping Cindy."

"I'm sorry I didn't protect you. I didn't keep my promise. I didn't stop the snowball," Riley said.

As I watched Riley embrace both Linda and Cindy, I realized, despite Riley's efforts, the snowball had not only crushed Riley, but covered his entire town.

Painful Decision

"It won't be much longer," I said, trying to comfort Johnny, though my heart beat rapidly. We were both waiting for the doctor to return and tell us the results of the latest round of tests. Johnny had taken a pretty bad fall off the roof of our house.

Because my wife was on a business trip, I was alone with Johnny as we awaited the doctor's return. I didn't need to see the tests to know that he was hurt pretty bad. I must have told him a thousand times to get off of that roof. But, I was doing some work on the roof toward the front of the house and he always wanted to be near me. He had been able to get on the roof by walking up a long plank that I had set up at the back of the house where the roof was not far from the ground.

I kept replaying the painful memory of seeing Johnny slip and fall off the roof. I shook my head trying to rid myself of the memory, but that was impossible as I looked at him lying on his stomach on top of the examining table. I think that was the only position he could be in where the pain was bearable. The doctor had given him pain medication as soon as he arrived, but I could tell that he was still hurting.

Sitting on the edge of the table, I gently massaged the back of his neck in an attempt to help him relax. It really hurt to see him like this. Johnny, with his cute face and short black hair, was 11 years old. He was always full of energy and was constantly begging to play a game, especially if it involved running. Ever since I sold my veterinary practice, I have spent much more time at home, allowing me to enjoy more quality time with Johnny.

Johnny certainly has had a tumultuous 11 years. He was taken from his biological parents shortly after his birth and given to an adoptive family. But that family abandoned him when he was five and I became the second person to adopt him, just 2 months after his abandonment. For the last eight years, I've basically been his dad, even though I think of him more as a best friend. I helped him through some pretty bad times and I have always cared for him as if he were my own flesh and blood.

But this situation was driving me crazy. I couldn't do anything to help him now. It was up to the doctors. Johnny glanced back at me as his trusting black eyes blinked slowly.

"It'll be okay," I said in as reassuring a tone as I could muster. Johnny turned back and rested his head on the table, apparently in too much pain to utter anything. I flashed back to some of the great times we had together, like when I would throw the ball with him in the park.

I quickly jerked my head around as I heard the door creak open. Dr. Roberts entered, holding a small stack of files. I had known Dr. Roberts, who was in his mid forties, for many years. As always, he appeared businesslike and professional. I jumped up and met him at the door. Johnny remained on the table.

"Will he be okay?" I whispered.

"I think so," he said, adjusting his eyeglasses. I put my right index finger up to my lips as an indication that I wanted him to lower his voice. Dr. Roberts rolled his eyes before whispering, "He has a few broken bones and a collapsed lung, but I think that he can make a full recovery with surgery."

"Surgery?" I repeated, hoping it wouldn't come to that. I grabbed Dr. Roberts by the arm and pulled him out of the room. "Surgery? Does this have anything to do with his heart?" I asked, referring to the fact that Johnny had been diagnosed with a degenerative heart condition a year ago.

"His heart wasn't damaged in the fall. His heart condition is the same as before. We can deal with that down the road. Right now, he needs the surgery to release the pressure from his lungs."

I folded my arms in front of my chest. "What kind of surgery are we talking about? And how painful will it be for Johnny?"

"I can't sugar-coat this, especially to you. It's a major surgery and he's going to be in some pain for awhile. But..."

"How long is awhile?"

He paused to scratch his head. "That's hard to say until we see how the surgery goes. But we may be talking just a few months if we're lucky."

Deep in thought, I simply stared at him. Finally, I spoke, "No, I don't want you to do the surgery. I don't want to put him through that kind of pain. He's had enough pain in his life."

"Hold on a minute. His lung has been damaged by the fall. It is causing him a great deal of pain right now. The pressure has to be released or he'll continue to be in great pain until he dies within a few days. He must get this surgery."

I paused for a moment. "Surgery and a painful recovery are the only ways he can make it through this?" He answered with a solemn nod. I took a deep breath and knew the painful decision that I had to make. "Then, forget it. No surgery."

"What?! Let me show you the x-rays."

"I don't want to see them," I said, holding my right hand up. "I need a few moments alone with Johnny."

Dr. Roberts paused before saying, "Of course." I went back into the room, closing the door behind me.

As I sat back down next to Johnny, a tear rolled down my face as I thought to myself, "He's not even a teenager yet." He was still lying on his stomach, remaining silent. For Johnny to be this still, I knew he had to be in a lot of pain. I was overwhelmed with grief and sadness. Abandoned earlier in life and diagnosed with a degenerative heart condition, which restricted some of his beloved activities, Johnny has had his share of suffering in his 11 years. I didn't want to see him suffer any more, through a painful surgery and a difficult recovery only to face a degenerative heart condition. I knew it was up to me to do something. I was his guardian. Now, I had to be his guardian angel.

I slowly pulled out a syringe of cyanide solution from my jacket pocket. After witnessing Johnny's fall, I knew it might come to this. I hoped it wouldn't, but it had. I believe that everyone who is good goes to heaven. And believe me, Johnny was good. I was going to send him to a better place, a place where he wouldn't have to suffer. I knew I was right. Still, my hands shook as I injected the cyanide into Johnny. He barely moved, figuring this was just another pain-killing shot. He didn't know that *this* shot would actually work.

I put the syringe on the counter and then wrapped my arms around him in a final embrace. I held onto him for at least five minutes before the door creaked open. It was Dr. Roberts.

"So, let's see how the patient is feeling," he said, approaching Johnny.

I walked to the other side of the room, knowing that I wouldn't be able to keep this from him. Tears flowed down my face as I watched him examine Johnny. He seemed momentarily stunned as he repeatedly checked for Johnny's pulse. He noticed the syringe on the counter and finally back to me.

"You did this?"

"It was for the best," I said, wiping away a stream of tears.

"No, it wasn't," he said, walking over to the syringe. He picked it up and shook his head. "You shouldn't have done this."

"I had to." My mouth quivered as I spoke. "I just couldn't continue to watch him suffer."

Dr. Roberts slumped back, resting his back on the counter with his arms folded at his chest. "You worked with me for three years. You trust me enough to take over your practice when you retired. Now, all of a sudden, you don't trust my medical judgment."

"This isn't about you." I walked back over to Johnny. With fresh new tears rolling down my face, I wrapped his body in the blankets in which I brought him. I did not turn around to look at Dr. Roberts as I said, "This is about what is best for Johnny. I did the right thing. He was getting very old."

"He was only 11 years old."

I turned around to look at Dr. Roberts. "You mean 77 years old," I said with raised eyebrows. There was an uncomfortable pause as he appeared speechless. "Come on doc, you know that a dog year is equivalent to seven human years." I picked up Johnny, who was like a son to me, and walked out of the veterinarian's office.

I Will Live Before I Die

"Ow!" I said silently to myself as I clutched my stomach. The pain was intense and I paused for a moment as I dropped to one knee. It felt like sharp needles were being rammed into my upper stomach just below my left ribs. After about five seconds, the pain subsided to a manageable level and I got up. I slowly made my way up the hill toward my high school. I squinted up at the overcast skies, which prevented any noticeable sunshine. I zipped up my jacket to protect myself from the early morning breeze and momentarily regretted my long-standing insistence on walking to school.

I'm seventeen years old and stand five feet eight inches with a body that one wouldn't call imposing. Everyone at my school knows that I'm not an athlete with my skinny frame. But, what only a handful of people know is that I'm suffering from leukemia. This disease has been with me just about my whole life, but it has seemingly gotten worse as of late, resulting in sudden weakness and unbearable stomach pains.

"We all have to play the cards that we're dealt. It's whether you make the most out of those cards that counts," my dad once told me. And that's what I try to remember every day. So I'm through the stage of feeling sorry for myself. I simply try to make each day the best day of my life- even if the day begins with intense stomach pains on a gloomy, chilly Monday morning.

At 8:20 in the morning, ten minutes before first period begins, I walked onto the noisy high school campus. The hallways were filled with students. The chattering of fellow students and the sounds of lockers being slammed shut bombarded my ears. I still held my aching stomach as I walked to my first period class. Just ten feet away was Jennifer Wright. The sight of her ravishingly good-looking body made me stop in my tracks.

Her perfect facial features complemented her beautiful black hair, which seductively dropped down to her shoulders. She was wearing that smile that used to melt my heart and caused my palms to get all sweaty and my mouth dry.

Jennifer was talking to her longtime boyfriend Max Reed, which reminds me that it has been two years since she asked me to the school dance. I was so happy I could barely sleep the night before the dance. Jennifer was my first love and she knew it. But, as it turned out, she had no intention of ever going with me. She was just using me to make Max jealous and left me at the entrance of the dance at the first sight of Max. I was crushed. I felt manipulated, betrayed, and completely dismissed. Somehow, my palms still get sweaty at the sight of her.

I must have been staring at her awhile as the memories of that dance flashed through my mind. Her pretty brown eyes met mine and she appeared offended that I was looking at her. As if to send me a message, she stood up on her tiptoes to give Max a long, sensuous kiss.

Max, being the school's star running back, was a tall, muscular guy. With big, broad shoulders and near perfect physique, Max fit the image around school as the ultimate tough guy. Depending upon on whether you ask the girls or the teachers at our high school, Max was either a hunk or a punk. I side with the latter.

He loved to push me around in front of his buddies while calling me "wimp" and "sissy". About a month ago when I was walking across the football field after school, Max fired the ball at me with all of his might. The point of the football hit the pit of my weakened stomach. I rolled on the ground in pain as Max laughed with his buddies.

This morning, he was wearing his red football jersey and faded blue jeans. I had often wondered whether those were the only clothes he owned.

Jennifer finally released her lips from Max. She glanced over at me wickedly. Max playfully ran his hands through her hair before taking off down the hallway.

I continued toward my class before Jennifer stepped in my path to say, "So what were you lookin' at?"

"Nothin'," I said, stepping around her. As I passed her, I muttered to myself, "Actually two nothings."

As I sat down for my first period class, the pain in my stomach eased because I was bent at the waist. Feeling a tap on my shoulder, I turned around in my chair. It was Susan Tolliver, the girl who sits right behind me in class. Susan had curly, brown hair that helped shape her round face. Now, I think I get along with most people. But, I disliked Susan. No, change that. I hated her.

"Robert," Susan said, pretending to be sincere. And I think that's what I really don't like about her. She pretends to be sincere. But, she's not. She lives for half-winged gossip and couldn't care less who she hurts with it. And she has hurt me many times. Once she spread it all around school that I was trying to steal Jennifer away from Max, provoking Max to beat me to a bloody pulp.

"So Robert, did you hear Mark Davidson didn't get into Berkeley or Stanford?" Susan asked in a whisper. "I hear that's the only schools he applied for." I simply stared dumbfounded at her as she smiled. She giggled. "He'll probably have to go to some community college."

I looked over at Mark who sat four rows over. Called "cute" by some girls, Mark had a boyish face and short blond hair. Mark was our high school's resident genius, according to Mark. He had an SAT score of 1560, but at age eighteen had yet to learn how to swim.

I have known Mark since grade school, but we never were what you would call "friends". For some reason, we always seemed to be competing against each other- from elementary school spelling bees to high school class elections. But, over the last year, the rivalry has gotten worse. About a year ago, because his mother worked as a nurse at my hospital, Mark found out that I had leukemia. Unlike Susan, it wasn't Mark's style to go telling everyone at school. Instead, he liked throwing it back in my face by sometimes ruthlessly calling me "Luke" rather than Robert. When you have leukemia, you never forget it. But every time Mark called me "Luke", it would give me a deep, spine chilling fear which can only come from having a fatal disease.

"So, are you hanging out with your girlfriend Jennifer on Catalina Island?" Susan sarcastically asked, breaking my concentration on Mark. She smiled broadly and started to giggle again.

Susan was referring to senior "ditch day" where the entire senior class got this Friday off to take a large chartered boat twenty-six miles to spend the day on Catalina Island.

I turned around and muttered, "She's not my girlfriend" as the school bell rang.

When I got home that day, the pain in my stomach got worse. I also felt a milder pain in the joints in my ankles and hip.

Finally, my parents rushed me to the emergency room. After what seemed like hours of X-rays, testing, and waiting, the doctor and my parents came into the room. The good news is the doctor was able to give me a shot earlier that greatly reduced the pain in my stomach. But, by the look of the three as they entered, some bad news was on the horizon. My mother's face appeared overwhelmed with grief. She wiped off a tear with a tissue that she pulled out of her purse. Alternatively eyeing my mother and then the floor, my dad was clearly having trouble looking at me.

"What's wrong?" The room was filled with silence. "If there's something wrong, I want to know."

My father nodded to the doctor, who turned and looked at me. "The tests that we have run have shown that the leukemia is not going into remission. The pain that you feel is from your spleen which is greatly swollen. And your other symptoms are consistent with what the X-rays..."

"Doc," I said, closing my eyes. "What's the bottom line?"

The doctor cleared his throat and adjusted his glasses as if to stall for time. Finally, he said, "I don't think you will live much more than a couple of months, and that's assuming you take it easy."

I was in shock and preoccupied with the phrase "couple of months to live". I asked to be left alone with my thoughts. The most prevalent thoughts were "Why me? And what did I do to deserve to die so young?" Of course, the answer was nothing. Some people live to be a hundred. Others die during childbirth. It's not fair. It's not right. It's life.

For my seventeen years, I always tried to do the right thing and live by the golden rule. Do unto others as you wish them to do unto you. And for the most part, it brought me love, happiness and respect from others. The glaring exception was four classmates: Jennifer, Max, Susan, and Mark.

Over the last four years, those four, in their own way, regularly belittled and disrespected me. Sometimes even making me feel less than human, like I didn't matter. I thought that if I was just nice to them that they would eventually be at least cordial in return, but four years of "turning the other cheek" had only given me a badly bruised face.

The thought that I would be dead soon and these other four would be able to continue living the next eighty years being mean and self absorbed left me angry. It actually infuriated me, so much so that I wanted to do something about it. I knew I couldn't convince them to change. They wouldn't listen to me. The only thing that I could do to stop them from behaving badly was to stop them from living.

If I was going to die young, they should go too. I knew this wasn't the right thing to do. But, sometime around three in the morning as I sat alone in the hospital room, I knew this is what I wanted to do. I had made my decision. I was going to live before I died.

I had all Monday night and all Tuesday morning to plan the murders of Jennifer, Max, Susan, and Mark. I didn't want to spend my last days in jail on murder charges. So, I knew I would have to do it in some secluded area with all of my adversaries present at the same time. I realistically felt this was impossible until I remembered the high school's Catalina trip this Friday.

The tradition is that the school rents a large boat to take all of the seniors to Catalina for a day of fun. My dad had a small cruise boat that I knew he'd let me use. If I offered my adversaries a boat ride to Catalina, they would almost certainly decline. But, I thought of a scheme to have all four of them miss the school boat. And guess who would happen to be there to take them to Catalina free of charge. Once on the boat far away from shore, I could then kill all four of them very quietly.

I didn't go to school again that week. My parents thought I stayed home to rest following doctor's orders. But, I was really home perfecting my plan. Late Thursday night, my dad and I locked up the boat at the dock. "I really don't think that you should be going out with your friends on the boat, it could be exhausting. Remember what the doctor said."

I put my hand on his shoulder. "Dad, I've been dealt some bad cards. But, I don't want to sit around and pout about it. I want to go out and have some fun. I'm trying to make the most of those cards. Isn't that what counts?"

My dad nodded his head before giving me a long hug.

My dad left later that night and I slept in the boat. At the front of the room is what I called the Captain's room. There was no furniture in the Captain's room other than a stool for the Captain to sit on. There was a counter just to the right of the ship's control. Behind the Captain's room were two cabins.

I woke up in the big cabin at seven o'clock in the morning to an absolutely beautiful day. There wasn't a cloud in the sky. As I stood outside on the deck, I looked out at the calm ocean. As the rising sun shone on the back of my neck, even my usually ailing body felt good. I was ready to *live*.

Everything went perfectly according to plan. The students began arriving at the main port at seven thirty for the eight o'clock departing time. At about 7:45, I put my plan into effect. I had gotten access to a small building near the port that didn't open until nine a.m. One by one, I called Jennifer, Max, Mark, and Susan over the loud speaker stating that each had an urgent phone call in building B. Once they arrived at Building B, I greeted them in full disguise wearing heavy makeup, hat, glasses, mustache, and beard. None of them recognized me. I led them each to a separate room and pointed inside where there was a phone off the hook. Once they went inside, I locked the door behind them.

With the 400 students in the senior class boarding the large boat, those four were never missed. And at 8:05, the boat took off leaving the four behind. I went back to the boat and changed clothes in addition to putting on some tight-fitting gloves. I threw my hat, glasses, mustache, and beard into the drawer by my revolver in the Captain's room underneath the counter.

I went back to Building B and quietly unlocked each of the doors. I then ran back toward the dock and waited for someone to come out of the building. As I waited, I was breathing hard from the run and I reminded myself that I needed to conserve my energy.

Shortly thereafter, all four of them figured out their doors were unlocked and came out of the building. Max started swearing up a storm when he realized that the boat had left. Jennifer was trying to calm Max down. Susan appeared in near tears and Mark seemed to be in deep thought trying to figure out what happened.

"It's show time," I said to myself. I walked over to the four and asked if they saw one of my closest friends from school. "I've got my dad's cruise boat and we were going to Catalina in it." The four fell for my bait- hook, line, and sinker. Max thought he "forced" me to take them to Catalina. Susan and Mark thought they had talked me into it. And Jennifer had the arrogance to think the love I felt for her two years ago did the trick.

After everyone boarded, I wasted no time in untying the rope, which docked the boat. Catalina was about a two-hour boat ride. I waited until we were almost an hour into our journey to call everyone into the Captain's room. I pulled out a cake, paper plates, a butcher's knife, a bottle of wine, and five wine glasses and placed them all on the counter next to the ships controls.

"What's all this?" Jennifer asked.

"A celebration," I replied.

"This is stupid," Mark said in his usual belittling tone. "You're offering us cake and wine at nine o'clock in the morning. You can be such an idiot."

"What's with the sissy gloves?" Max asked, his arm wrapped around Jennifer.

"It's to keep my hands from getting dirty," I responded, before asking Mark to cut the cake.

"Cut the cake with this?" Mark asked, picking up the 12-inch butcher's knife.

"Sorry. That's all I have."

Mark shook his head and began to cut the cake, mumbling, "It figures, Luke."

"Luke?" Susan asked, as a sharp chill went down my spine.

"It's a nickname," Mark said, looking at me with a sinister smile. I responded to Mark with a hateful glare.

"How did he get that nickname?" Susan asked, cozying up to Mark. "I gotta know."

"It's not important," I said, handing Susan the wine bottle while keeping one eye on the sea.

"Someone's a little sensitive about their nickname," Susan said in a teasing tone. "Aren't you, Luke?"

"Just pour please," I said to Susan.

"Tell me later," Susan whispered to Mark as she poured the wine into the five glasses. What she did not know was that one of the glasses already had a lethal amount of arsenic. I chipped that glass at its base so I could identify it.

Max took his arm off Jennifer and approached me. "All you have is wine!" Max blurted out, shoving me to make sure he had my attention. I fell back, banging my left hip against the counter. I winced. "Don't you have any beer?" I answered by shaking my head. "Nice going, sissy boy."

All of the times that Max had physically hurt me flashed through my mind. Despite the pain in my hip, I managed to smile. "Please, try the wine," I said, handing Max the chipped glass.

Everyone else took a glass but Mark, who put his hands up. "I'm not having any of your stupid wine."

"Hold it for the toast," I said to him. Mark relented and I began the toast. "Let's not kid ourselves. I haven't really been a close friend with any of you. In fact, if you hadn't missed the school's boat, none of you would even be here. But, I think in life, everything happens for a reason. And right now, right here, we're all together. And that…"

"Can you get on with it?" Jennifer asked, rolling her eyes.

I calmly nodded my head, but boiled inside, angry that she interrupted my big moment. I looked at everyone else's eyes. It was clear that no one wanted to listen to me talk. I raised my glass and succinctly said, "May we all lead happy, long lives after we graduate." With that, everyone besides Mark drank. Max, finishing his drink all in one shot, complained again about the lack of beer, blinked his eyes and dropped to the floor.

"Are you okay?" Jennifer asked, reaching down to check on Max.

"I don't feels so good," Max mumbled in slurred speech.

"He's drunk," I said softly to Mark and Susan. I took a moment to admire the big, tough football player knocked to the ground because of me.

"Never heard of anyone getting drunk on one glass of wine," Mark said with assurance.

My hands started to shake. I suddenly felt dizzy and weak. This sudden stress was exactly what I didn't need. "Uh, you never know how much he had before he came," I muttered.

With that, Mark and Jennifer helped a dying Max into the small cabin. "One down, three to go," I said to myself.

I continued to direct the boat from the Captain's room, waiting to hear the news that Max was dead. I was rehearsing my reaction and response. My mood was mixed. On one hand, I felt a sense of achievement, conquering my most physically intimidating adversary. On the other hand, I had already begun to feel tired and for the first time today, I felt a slight pain in my stomach.

As I sat down on the stool, I tried to recuperate. For a moment, I was able to appreciate the beauty of the sea and soak in the warmth of the sunshine. The ocean was calm today and there wasn't another boat in sight on this early weekday morning.

"Robert," Mark said, entering the Captain's room. "I was just with Jennifer and Max. Something is seriously wrong with him. Maybe we should turn back."

"We'll be at Catalina soon. We'll get him help there." I knew I had to free myself from directing the boat and I felt I could trick Mark into taking over. "It's pretty hard driving this thing, but I learned it pretty quickly."

"Can't be that hard. And if you can do it, I certainly can." Mark pushed me over. "Show me how!" I showed him the controls and he caught on quickly. "Ah, this is a piece of cake," Mark said smugly. "I can handle this by myself."

I acted concerned, but I let him talk me into it. I slowly walked toward the back of the boat where Susan was staring out at the ocean. "Hey Susan," I whispered. "I think I know what happened to Max." When she leaned close to me, I knew I had her full attention. "I think Mark tried to poison Max. Remember, Mark was the only one who refused to drink any wine."

"That's right," Susan said in agreement. Her eyes lit up, thinking she was privy to some inside information. I enjoyed duping Susan with of all things- gossip!

"I think I have a cell phone around here somewhere. I want you to keep an eye on Mark in the Captain's room. I'm going to try to reach a hospital in Catalina for Max." As Susan walked to the Captain's room, I pretended that I was going in the big cabin. But, as soon as Susan entered the Captain's room, I sneaked out and headed to the small cabin.

When I opened the door, I was surprised at what I saw. Sitting on the bed, Jennifer was in tears as she held Max. "He's dead!" Jennifer said, trying to wipe away the tears that were smearing her makeup. I had to admit I felt bad. Not that I killed Max, but that I had made Jennifer cry. I didn't enjoy seeing her so sad. I slowly walked up to her thinking that I had to put her out of her misery. "Just get out of here!" Jennifer cried, burying her head into Max's large shoulders.

I closed my eyes. I remembered how I felt the night of the dance two years ago as I reached into my coat pocket for a syringe full of arsenic. "It'll all be over soon," I said as I sat down on the edge of the bed beside Jennifer who was still clinging to a lifeless Max. I took a deep breath and quickly covered Jennifer's mouth with my left hand and jammed the syringe into her left arm. I held her tightly for the next couple of minutes. As I held her, I closed my eyes and pretended we were dancing. I think she owed me a dance. I looked at her pale, yet attractive face and then into her beautiful, brown eyes. She was pretty. In fact, drop dead gorgeous, I snickered to myself. I finally let go of her lifeless body and let her fall into Max's arms. After all, that's where she always wanted to be.

I left the room, closing the door behind me. I'm not sure if it was the physical or emotional toll of killing Jennifer, but I suddenly felt very tired. With all of my activity, the joints in my knees and ankles had become sore. I wanted to lie down and rest, but I still had work to do. I gingerly walked to the back of the boat and began to pour a gallon of water into the boat's gas tank, which I knew would stall the boat. I then slowly walked to the Captain's room where Susan and Mark were chatting away. "No luck! I can't find my cell phone," I announced. I turned to Mark. "I wanted to call a hospital on Catalina so an ambulance could meet us when we arrive."

"That's Catalina Island straight ahead," Susan said pointing. "We can't be more than 45 minutes away."

"I'll speed up and make that 30 minutes," Mark said, still controlling the ship. As Mark tried to speed up, the engine began to stall. Apparently, the water was beginning to have an effect on the engine. The boat jerked a little, then slowly came to halt. "What's going on?" Mark asked frantically.

"I don't know," I said lying. "What did you do?"

"Nothing! This boat's a piece of crap." I pushed Mark out of the way and pretended to try to restart the boat. As I tried, I sat down on the stool feeling physically exhausted. I started to feel increasing pain in my stomach.

"Oh my gosh! If the ship won't start, how will we get Max help?" Susan turned toward me and asked, "How's he doing?"

I had to pause a moment to clear my mind. The joints in my ankle, knee, and hip all ached, but I had to forget my physical ailments and refocus on my task. "I don't know. I've been looking for my cell phone in the other cabin."

"I'll check on Max," Mark said, before running out of the Captain's room.

"Why can't you get it started?" Susan asked with a concerned look on her face.

"I think someone has made sure I can't," I said, giving Susan a serious look.

"What do you mean? Who?"

"Well, who was the last one working these controls?"

"Mark," Susan said softly in deep thought.

At that moment, Mark rushed back in the Captain's room saying, "What's going on here?"

"What?" I asked.

"It's Max," Mark replied. "He's dead too."

"What do you mean too?" Susan asked.

"Jennifer is dead," Mark said with his eyes darting from Susan back to me. I could tell that Mark's mind was racing. But, I didn't think he had figured anything out, at least not yet.

Susan raced out of the room, apparently headed to check on Jennifer. That left Mark and me alone in the Captain's room. "Did you kill Jennifer?" Mark asked bluntly.

"Of course not," I said, reaching for the cake and the butcher's knife. As I held the knife in my right hand, Mark jumped back. "Oh give me a break," I said, trying to laugh despite the intense pain in my stomach. I couldn't have killed a guarded Mark even if I wanted to. I simply didn't have the strength. Besides, he was much stronger than me even if I didn't feel physically sick. "I'm going to lock this up. It could be used as a weapon." I slowly walked out of the Captain's room and into the vacant small cabin. I wanted to finish my original mission, but I needed to rest. I set the cake and knife on the nightstand and collapsed on the bed. I curled up in the fetal position, which helped ease the pain in my stomach. I laid on the bed with my eyes open. I feared if I closed them and fell asleep, I'd never wake up.

I rested for what seemed like three minutes when Susan raced in the cabin and locked the door behind her. She breathed a sigh of relief as if the weight of the world was released from her shoulders. But when Susan turned around, her relief disappeared because she could tell that I was in pain. "Oh my gosh!" she said dropping down to one knee to get a closer look at me. "What's wrong?"

"My stomach, it hurts," I said, actually telling the truth.

Susan spotted the butcher's knife and cake next to me. "Tell me you didn't eat any of the cake recently." I quickly realized where Susan's mind was going, so I decided to play along. I nodded my head. "How could you be so stupid?"

At that moment, someone began knocking hard on the door. Then, Mark's voice shouted, "Susan! Open this door! For all of our safety, we have to stay together!"

"Forget it!" Susan yelled back. "I'll be safe locked in here."

"Is Robert in there?!" Mark asked, still yelling.

"Yes, he is."

"Then, you better get out of there!" Mark screamed as he pounded on the door. "Open the door!"

"Listen!" Susan shouted, standing up and turning toward the door. "There's no way I'm opening this door. So, just forget it!"

It was clear Susan was convinced Mark was the killer and I was harmless. In fact, I think she thought I was dying. And she may have been right because I felt worse than had ever had in my life. I had lost almost all of my energy. Worse yet, my legs were getting numb. It felt like the leukemia had simply taken over my entire body.

"Fine!" Mark said, apparently walking away from the door.

"You said that there was a cell phone in this room," Susan said, facing me. "We have to find it so we can call for help." So that's her plan, I thought. Too bad it wasn't going to work because there never was a cell phone on the boat. I had made it up.

Susan began frantically looking in the drawers of the nightstand. As she looked, I tried to get my mind to focus back on my mission. How was I going to kill Susan and Mark? Both were stronger than me, especially Mark. I knew the easiest and possibly only way was to get to the revolver. But that was all the way back in a drawer in the Captain's room. And that seemed way too far to travel now. I massaged my numb legs. I was unsure whether I could get up if I tried. And I didn't want to try.

"It's not in here," Susan finally said, slamming one of the nightstand's drawers shut. She walked over to me. When I didn't move, Susan grabbed and pulled me off the bed allowing me to fall to my knees leaning up against the nightstand. I slumped to the ground as my right hand rested on the nightstand.

"I don't know about you. But I'm not going to die on this stupid boat," Susan said, frantically walking back over to the bed. I desperately fought the temptation to close my eyes, like a child who was fighting to stay awake to see the late show on television. At that point, my hand brushed up against a soft, gooey substance on the nightstand. What was that? Oh, I know. It was the icing on the cake. "Hey, you ever take your girlfriend Jennifer out on this boat before?" Susan asked, now on top of the bed, which was up against the wall. She was feeling on the other side of the bed to see if the phone had fallen into that crevasse.

I boiled in anger blurting out, "She was not my girlfriend!" A flash quickly came to me. If my hands were close to the cake, the butcher's knife must be close by. A shot of energy manifested in anger and hatred spread through my body. I tilted my head up and looked at the top of the nightstand and spotted the knife.

"Huh?" Susan said, not understanding me and not even turning around. If she had, she would have seen me grab the knife and stumble towards her. With rage as my only energy left, I plunged the knife into Susan's back. She let out a slight scream and fell on the bed, and I fell to the floor.

It took me over five minutes to gather the strength to get up. In those five minutes, I didn't hear anything from Susan. When

I struggled to my feet, I could see Susan lying face down on the bed with the knife still implanted in her back. I chuckled at the symbolism. Only one left, I thought. Then, I could rest forever. I had to get to the revolver in the Captain's room. I wondered whether I could get to it with Mark somewhere on the boat. But, I knew I had nothing to lose. I had to try. My legs were now very numb and I found it difficult to stand. But as I did stand upright, a searing pain ran through my stomach. I struggled to walk to the door of the cabin. As I stumbled toward the door, I bent over in an attempt to lessen the pain. I quietly unlocked the door and slowly walked out.

As soon as I stepped out of the cabin, I was grabbed and thrown up against the side of the boat. I cried out in agony as pain ripped through my stomach. "You slimeball!" Mark yelled. With nostrils flaring, his face turned beet red with anger. "Look what I found!" he said, showing me the revolver. I closed my eyes in frustration. Mark pressed the gun up against the side of my head. "Wait, there's more. Look what else I found." Still holding the revolver to my head with his right hand, he yanked out of his jacket pocket with his left hand my disguise- my beard and glasses. "It was you in that building! You planned for us to miss the school boat so that you could lure us onto this boat!" He threw the disguise down and grabbed my shirt near my chest with his left land and twisted. "You were probably planning to kill all of us! But, I'm too smart for you. You got that Luke!" Mark screamed, shoving me back against the outside wall of the cabin. He looked into my eyes, feeling powerful and in control.

"Susan!" Mark shouted. "Get out here! I've got our murderer." There was a dead silence. "Susan!" Mark looked back at me. I was in too much pain to smile, but I did raise my eyebrows, which conveyed the message. "You didn't," Mark said, dragging me back into the cabin to see Susan's corpse still lying on the bed with a knife in her back.

Mark didn't take long to mourn Susan's death. He quickly dragged me back to the Captain's room. Once in the room, he violently threw me on the floor, busting my lip open.

"You always had a temper when things don't go your way," I muttered.

"Shut up!" Mark ordered. He patted me down to see if I had any weapons. When he felt a relatively large bulge in my jacket, he pulled out the syringe that killed Jennifer. "Look what we have here." He put the syringe in the top drawer.

As I lay there on the floor, I was ready to give up. Mark had won. I guess he was right. He was smarter than me. "Okay," Mark said, aiming the revolver at me. "I know there's a way to send a distress signal. Either tell me or I'll shoot you now."

"You think death scares me," I mumbled, tasting my own blood from my busted lip.

"Who said I was going to kill you," Mark said, holding the gun now with both hands. "I'll make you suffer. I'll shoot you in one leg, then in an arm, then in your crotch."

"Okay, you win," I said, too exhausted to get up. "On the control board, the top row, third button from the left, the button marked 'distress'. It sends out a distress signal. The Coast Guard should be here in less than twenty five minutes."

Mark pushed the button and then leaned back against the counter with the revolver still pointing at me. What he didn't know was that was unnecessary. I didn't have the strength to get up. "You know, you're a real sicko! You get us on this boat. You act like nothing is wrong, offering us wine and cake. You have me cutting the cake for Pete's sake. You're making toasts..."

"That's right, you were the one who cut the cake," I said, somehow finding the strength to giggle.

"What's so funny?" Mark asked, dropping the revolver down to his side. "So I cut the cake, so what?"

"Nothin'," I said, still chuckling. I realized I had finished my mission. I had lived before I died. The only thing left now was to die.

"You're a psycho!" Mark looked back out for the Coast Guard for a moment, then his eyes fixed back on me.

I slowly and deliberately took my gloves off. Mark did see me, but he didn't see any harm in it. I reached into my pocket and pulled out my small vial of arsenic that I used to kill Max. There wasn't much left. I hoped it would be enough. When Mark looked away, I quickly downed the remaining arsenic. Now, it was just a matter of minutes before I was dead. I put the empty vial in one of the gloves, rolled both gloves into a ball and threw them through the open door to the Captain's room and out to sea.

"What was that?!" Mark spun around, aiming the gun at me.

"Wanna know why I's did it?" I muttered, ignoring Mark's question. I shook my head in a vain attempt to clear my mind.

"No!" Mark replied, dropping the gun back down to his side.

"Revenge," I mumbled anyway.

"Well, you didn't get revenge against me," Mark said, strongly pointing the revolver back at me.

"Life in prisin for killin fo peoples revenge enough," I mumbled in slurred speech.

"What? What are you talking about?"

I didn't bother to explain. I'm not sure if it was the leukemia or the arsenic, but I was unable to talk. I felt my eyes blink uncontrollably, and my heart rate soar. But my mind was serene, and my final thoughts were of Mark, who in the end was not smart enough to realize that the only fingerprints on the butcher's knife and the syringe would be his...

Murder in the Suburbs

As I pulled into my friend Adam's driveway, my thoughts were consumed with my wife. Although I had been looking forward to this fishing trip for several months, I couldn't stop thinking about what I was leaving behind. I've been married for eight years. For the last two, we never have stopped arguing. We argued about household chores, money, raising our kids, and most recently, this fishing trip.

I got out of my car and Adam walked out of the house to meet me. We have been best friends since junior high school. Knowing him for almost twenty years, I recognized that look on his face. I was about to get an earful. "Where have you been? You live just ten minutes away and you're twenty minutes late."

I looked at my watch, which read 9:17. "Fifteen minutes late and I had to stop for gas." A meticulous planner when it came to our fishing trips, he liked keeping to a schedule. It was a trait that drove me crazy. "I'm sure the fish will still be there once we arrive."

Adam didn't even smile, which told me he wasn't done complaining. "I called you on your cell phone a little while ago, but you didn't pick up."

"You did?" I said, reaching into my car. I looked at my cell phone, which displayed the message. "Missed call: 9:05". I scratched my head. "I must have been inside the mini mart paying for the gas."

"If you don't keep your phone with you, what's the point of having one?" Adam asked, loading his luggage and gear into my car. I chose not to respond. With the constant battles I have had with my wife, I was not about to be suckered into an argument with Adam.

As he continued to vent, I let my mind shift back to thoughts of my wife. After a few minutes on the road, his venting finally ceased and he began talking about a recent case. Diligent and intelligent, Adam had worked his way up to senior deputy in his county's police department. He loved talking about his job. Usually, I liked listening to it, but I really wasn't interested today. I had enough drama in my life. "What's the matter with you? You haven't said a word in the last five minutes. You okay?"

I looked at him for a moment and then back at the road. "It's Marilyn."

"What's the matter?"

"She works late almost every night. And when I do see her, we argue all the time."

"About what?"

"Everything. This morning, it was about this trip."

"She's upset that she has the kids all weekend?"

"That's the thing," I said, thumping the steering wheel. "She doesn't even have the kids. They're at my parents."

"So, what's she doing this weekend?"

"I don't know. Some girls weekend thing."

Adam lightly punched my upper arm. "Hang in there. Everything with your marriage is going to work out. Trust me."

"So, the single guy is an expert on marriage," I said, smiling.

"I may not know much about marriage, but I do know you and Marilyn. You'll make it through this." Adam was an eternal optimist. The glass was always half full in his eyes.

I looked at the clock on the dashboard. "Hey, it's ten o'clock. The football game just came on."

"What station?"

"I don't know. Just use the scan button." With the radio turned on the AM dial, Adam hit scan. We listened in silence, patiently waiting for the sounds of the football game.

The parade of unfamiliar voices gave way to a woman who said, "I just don't know what to do. I think my marriage may be over."

A chill went down my spine. My eyes widened as I recognized the voice on the radio. I couldn't believe my ears. "That's Marilyn," I said, pulling the car over to the side of the road.

Adam had recognized the voice as well and had pushed the scan button again so the radio remained on that station. He turned the volume up.

"Hold on caller," the female host said. "I want you to take a deep breath." At that moment, another phone rang on the radio. "Karen, I want you to ignore everything else, including that other call. I'll need you to focus."

"She called her Karen," Adam said with a perplexed look. "Are you sure it's Marilyn?"

"Yeah, she's just using a fake name," I said, before waving him off to be quiet.

"Now, Karen, I want to start from the beginning. How long have you been married?"

There was a momentary pause on the radio before Marilyn said, "Eight years."

Adam said, "This is so weird…"

"Shhh!!" I said, unable to believe I was listening to my wife's voice on the radio.

"So, what's the problem with your marriage?" the talk show host asked.

"For the last two months, I have been having an affair. My husband has no idea."

I looked over to Adam, his jaw dropped. I put my hand up to my forehead and slowly shook my head.

"Now, why did you have an affair?" the talk show host asked. "I mean, what would make you break your wedding vows?"

"I don't know. My wedding vows mean everything to me. My kids mean everything to me. It was stupid, having an affair for two months. I want to stop because I still love my husband. I don't want my marriage to end." Marilyn sniffled. "I want to be with my husband."

"So, what are you going to do?" There was silence on the radio for a moment before the host said, "Are you there? What are you going to do?"

"My God, no. Don't! Ahk!" Then, the dead air returned.

"Hello caller. What's going on? Are you there? Hello." Still, no response. My heartbeat quickened. "Did she hang up?" the host asked his call screener. "I'm being told that the line is still active. Ma'am, no one is judging you. Please talk to us." Again, dead air filled the radio. "Okay, this is a good time to take a break and we'll try to get that caller back on the line." The station cut to a commercial. I sat motionless.

"Man, are you okay?" Adam asked. I looked at him, not knowing what to say. "Did you hear how that ended?"

I stared at the radio dial, lost in my own thoughts. "She's been cheating on me for two months."

"Snap out of it," Adam said. "I'm worried about Marilyn. Call her on your cell phone."

"And say what?" I said, slowly picking up the phone. "Why is she cheating on me?"

"Forget about that for a moment. I want to make sure she's okay."

I dialed my home number and the phone rang a few times before it went to voicemail. I thrust the phone in his direction so he could hear our recorded voicemail greeting.

"Call her cell phone," Adam said.

I dialed her cell phone. I shook my head as I looked at Adam. "There's no answer."

The radio program came back from commercial break and the host said, "Unfortunately, we could not get back in touch with our last caller. Ma'am, stay strong and fight for your marriage. You're free to call back here any time. Let's go to our next caller."

"Something's not right," Adam said, lowering the volume on the radio. "I've got a bad feeling about this." He pulled out his cell phone and dialed a number. "This is deputy Adam Monroe. I need to get a squad car out to…" Adam said my address. I was in too much of a daze, too paralyzed to speak or act. I just listened to Adam. "A call just came from that residence and it sounded suspicious. Now, the woman is not picking up the phone. I think something may have happened to her. Someone needs to check it out ASAP. We have the consent of the owner to go in if no one answers."

After wrapping up his call, Adam looked at me. "What are you waiting for? Turn off at the next exit and let's get back to your house." I nodded and we started our trek back home.

When I turned the corner onto my street, I noticed four police cars surrounding the front of my house. Their lights were flashing and a lot of curious neighbors were out on their front porch. Adam and I jumped out of the car and jogged toward the group of officers standing on the front porch.

"What's going on?" Adam asked one of his fellow officers. "This is my friend. He lives here."

"Have you seen my wife? Is she okay?"

There was a pause before one of the female officers stepped forward. "I'm Sheriff Reid. Why don't you have a seat?" In her mid forties, she wore a beige uniform, which prominently displayed a star-shaped sheriff's badge. She struck me as an experienced and trusted officer of the law as her outstretched hand pointed toward one of the chairs on my front porch.

I slowly sat down. "Tell me. What's going on?" I asked, even though I already knew.

In a very unemotional, businesslike tone, she said, "We found a woman stabbed to death on the kitchen floor. We believe it's your wife."

"My God," Adam said, putting his hand on my shoulder.

I paused for a moment not knowing what to say. All eyes were on me as if they were waiting for some kind of reaction. "I want to see the woman," I said.

"No, let me," Adam said. Before I knew it, he headed inside. He returned about a minute later.

"Well?" I said, standing up.

He didn't say anything at first. He just gave me a big bear hug. As we embraced, he whispered, "I'm sorry. I'm so sorry."

Adam slowly escorted me back to the car. As we walked, he said, "The police are going to have some questions for you. Do you feel up to answering them?"

I nodded, but my mind was really miles away. Once we reached my car, I leaned up against it as I put both hands on my head. The nearby sights and sounds mesmerized me: flashing patrol cars, curious neighbors, and the large contingent of people entering and exiting my home. I was going through the full range of emotions: anger, guilt, fear, and helplessness.

"Michael, you with me?" Adam asked as he touched my shoulder. "I'm going to let the sheriff know that I'm taking you down to the station. Stay here, okay?"

I nodded again before I watched Adam jog back toward the house.

"Michael!" a voice said from behind me.

I turned around and saw my next-door neighbor Hal approaching. Hal, a single man in his mid twenties, worked as a personal trainer at a local gym.

Wearing shorts and a t-shirt, he said, "What's going on? Is everything okay?"

"No," I said, shaking my head for emphasis.

"Oh man. Is Marilyn alright?"

I paused for a moment, wondering what to say. Hal was not what I would call a friend. But, I have been over to his house to watch a game and Marilyn and I have had him over for dinner. I opted to tell him the truth. "She's dead. Someone murdered her."

Hal's jaw dropped and his hand quickly covered his mouth. He was speechless.

"Hey Hal!" Adam said as he approached us. "You see anyone around this house about forty five minutes ago."

Hal rubbed his face, apparently still absorbing the shocking news. "No, uh not really," Hal said stuttering. "I...I think I was back from cycling by then, but I didn't notice anyone."

"That's too bad," Adam said. He turned and looked at me. "Okay. Let's go. I'll drive." He held his hand out for my keys.

I dropped the keys in his hand and walked around the car to the passenger's side. As I passed Hal, he muttered, "I'm so sorry about Marilyn." I nodded as I got into my car.

I waited in the police station for about twenty minutes. During that time, Adam and I tried to replay Marilyn's last words on the radio. He was trying to remember any details that might give us a clue to who killed her.

The door opened and Sheriff Reid walked in. "Mr. Blake, I can't tell you how sorry I am about your wife. She was twenty-nine years old. Had her whole life ahead of her." I looked at her not knowing what to say. So, I remained silent. Sheriff Reid sat down and opened up a file. She then turned toward Adam and said, "If you would excuse us, I need to talk to Michael alone."

"Of course," Adam said. He patted me on the shoulder before leaving.

Sheriff Reid leaned forward over the table. "I want you to know I am going to do everything in my power to get the guy who did this." I nodded to acknowledge her pledge. "I have some important questions for you. I'm hoping your answers might help us."

"Sure," I said, straightening up in my chair.

"Exactly when was the last time you saw your wife?"

I stopped to think for a moment. "A little before 9:00 AM, I left to go to Adam's house. We were going on a fishing trip. That was the last time I saw her. I heard her about an hour later on the radio. She had called into a talk show."

"Yes, Adam mentioned that to me," the sheriff said, stroking her chin. She looked down at her files as she said, "It does not appear that your wife was killed by a robber. There was no forced entry into your house. There were valuables, like jewelry, left on your wife and expensive china around the house."

"So, what are you saying?"

"I'm saying that I believe that this wasn't a random act of violence. Someone wanted to kill her. Can you think of any reason someone would want to hurt her?"

"No," I said, shaking my head.

After ten more minutes of questions, the sheriff ended the session. Adam escorted me out of the police station and back toward the car. "So, what do you want to do?" he asked as we reached the car. "I'll drive you wherever you want."

"Just take me to your house. I need to make some phone calls to Marilyn's family and friends."

"You got it," Adam said as we got into his car. "While you're doing that, I'm going to find the sicko that did this. He's out there somewhere thinking he got away with it."

Once Adam dropped me off at his house, I began the task of notifying family and friends. I had grown to love Marilyn's family and many of her close friends. Being the messenger of the worst possible news was extremely difficult. And it did not get easier with each phone call.

That night, Adam brought home take-out. After we sat down to eat, I asked him for an update.

"We made some progress. A lot of progress."

"Really," I said, raising my eyebrows.

"Yeah. We completed our search of the house. We found some love letters addressed to Marilyn." Adam paused for a moment and tilted his head slightly. "Michael, they weren't from you."

A lump formed in my throat. "Who were they from?"

"Hal."

"Hal? My next door neighbor?" Adam nodded and I fell back in my chair. "My God, I can't believe he... So, Marilyn was having an affair with him?"

"I think so," Adam said. "They were clearly love letters, not friendship notes." Adam wiped his lips with a napkin. "We found them in a box in the bottom drawer of her dresser."

I shook my head as I gnashed my teeth so hard they began to hurt. "You know, on the radio, she said that she was having an affair, but she was going to come back to me. The call ended abruptly. Maybe she was murdered on the air by Hal out of jealousy."

"It's a good theory. I thought of it too," Adam said. "The hard thing is to prove it."

"Well, what other progress have you made?"

"We retrieved the tape of the radio talk show," Adam said, pulling a CD about of his pocket.

I sat up in my chair. "I want to hear it."

"You will, but hold on," Adam said. "I'm convinced that she was murdered on this tape. That puts her death right at about 10:07. Hal told us that he went biking in the morning with some friends. We interviewed his cycling buddies. He was done by 9:40 and drove back home. Hal admits to being home alone by 10:00, right next door.

"He had opportunity as well as motive. You gotta arrest him."

Adam shook his head. "You have to be patient. The sheriff wants to get the rest of the physical evidence from the lab. Should be in tomorrow morning."

"I want to listen to Marilyn's call." Adam played the CD. It was about six minutes in length, counting the commercial break.

When the CD ended, Adam said, "You heard the phone ring during the conversation. On the way home, I think I figured it out. I think that was Marilyn's cell phone."

"Yeah, so?"

"Well, picture this. Hal sees you leave, so he calls Marilyn. When she doesn't answer, he comes by the house. He lets himself in and overhears Marilyn talking on the phone saying she is devoted to you. He snaps and stabs her."

I nodded slowly, impressed with Adam's logic. "Can I have that CD? I'd like to listen to it a few more times. I want to see if I can pick up anything else."

"Sure," Adam said, handing it to me. "It's a copy."

"It's amazing how life changes in an instant. I've lost my wife, forever." I dropped my head and fought back the tears. "You know it's true what they say. You never fully appreciate how important someone is until they're gone."

"Listen to me," Adam said, looking directly at me. "I can't bring Marilyn back. But, I promise you that I will make sure the person that killed Marilyn rots in jail. I will not rest until I make this right, I promise."

When I woke up the next morning, I turned over to embrace Marilyn. Reality set in as my arm landed with a thud against the mattress. My heart sunk and tears began to roll down my face. I turned back over to look at the clock, which read 8:15. I slowly walked out of Adam's guest room and looked for him. I found a note in the kitchen saying he was going into the station early.

Alone in Adam's house, I spent most of the morning talking to family members to assure them I was okay.

I was putting on a brave front for everyone. But, in reality, I was missing the love of my life terribly. I would do anything to bring her back. It was Sunday morning and I got in my car and drove to my church. Father Mike presided over the mass. An older, slender priest with white hair and glasses, he has known me for over three years. He was a friend and spiritual leader to both Marilyn and me.

After mass, I spent some time talking to him about everything, including exactly what happened to my wife, my regrets for all the things I did and didn't do, and how to proceed from here. It felt good to open up to him about everything that had happened.

"I don't know who I can trust any more. I knew Marilyn and I had our problems, but I never thought she would go behind my back like that. And I had no idea. How could I be so oblivious? How could I think she still loved me?"

"There is something you should know," Father Mike said. "Marilyn came to see me several times. She told me about the affair, but she also told me that she loved you very much. She was sorry for what she had done." I sniffled as he talked, trying to avoid a full outburst of tears. "She made a terrible mistake, but she was going to try to make it right. Perhaps, you can learn something from that."

As Father Mike talked, my mind became consumed with the knowledge that he knew about Marilyn's infidelity. "Father, do you know who she had the affair with?"

There was a momentary silence before he said, "I can't disclose the details of a confession, even a confession of the deceased."

"Of course," I said, feeling ashamed.

"You should be more focused on healing yourself. Ask God for forgiveness for your sins and pray on how you can live a more Christian life."

"Yes father," I said nodding. "I will."

After leaving church around noon, I called Adam at the police station, hoping to hear that they had Hal in custody. Even without Father Mike's disclosure, I was convinced that Hal was the one who had the affair with Marilyn.

"Hey, Michael, how are you doing?" Adam said, recognizing my cell phone number.

"Fine. You get the physical evidence from the lab?"

"Yeah," Adam said slowly.

"And… did you arrest Hal?"

There was momentary pause before Adam said, "No."

"Why not?"

"Evidence shows he didn't murder Marilyn. It would have been impossible."

"Impossible? What are you talking about? Wasn't he having an affair with Marilyn?"

"Yeah, we think he was."

"You *think*?"

Adam sighed. "All we really have to go on are those love notes. And we don't really know when they were written."

Adam's words were making my head spin. "Hold on a minute. What makes you think it's impossible for Hal to be the murderer? He admitted to being right next door at the time of her death."

"Look, I can't go into it right now. The sheriff wants me to check on something. We can talk about it tonight. I'll be home at five o'clock." Adam hung up the phone abruptly. I sat for a few moments in shock as I listened to the dial tone.

Five o' clock came and went as I waited for Adam. By six o'clock, I began to get restless and called his cell phone. There was no answer. I decided to call the police station.

"Hello, this is Michael Blake. I am looking for Deputy Adam Monroe."

"Hold on one moment," the operator said.

There was about a twenty-second delay before a voice came on the phone. "Hello, Mr. Blake, this is Sheriff Reid."

"Oh, hi. I was looking for Adam."

"So am I. He left around one o'clock to get something for me and I haven't seen him since. You haven't talked to him today after one o'clock, have you?"

"No, I haven't. Since I have you on the phone sheriff, can you give me an update on the investigation?"

"It's going well. In fact, we just fixed the time of death. It wasn't 10:07 AM. It was 9:07 AM."

"No, no. That can't be right. I heard her on the radio after ten o'clock. She was clearly alive."

"Yes, but the show wasn't live. It was on one-hour tape delay. We confirmed it with the station."

I paused a moment and a ton of thoughts raced through my mind. "Are you sure?"

"Yes, we also cross checked it with the phone company records. It shows a call on your home line to the station from 8:55 to 9:07. Mr. Blake, your wife wasn't on the phone when you left, was she?"

"No, she walked with me out to the car. She gave me a hug and a kiss goodbye in the driveway."

"So anyone watching your house would have seen you leave and known Marilyn was in the house?" Sheriff Reid asked.

"Yeah."

"Her murder happened so soon after you left. It's as if someone was waiting for you to leave. Who knew you were going away that morning?"

"I don't know who Marilyn told, but I only told my parents and Adam."

"Well, I appreciate your patience with my many questions. I hope to have more information for you as soon as I can catch up with Adam. He was following up on a lead."

"Okay," I said. "Thanks."

As soon as I hung up the phone, I heard the garage door open. I walked out to the living room to greet Adam. As he walked in from the garage, the shirt on his beige police uniform was uncharacteristically untucked. He looked exhausted.

"Where have you been?" I asked. "It's 6:15. You said you'd be home by five."

"You should have a seat," Adam said, pointing to the couch. "We need to talk."

"Okay," I slowly said before taking a seat on the couch. Adam sat down in a nearby chair. "Where have you been?" I asked again. "Even the sheriff didn't know where you were."

"I've been gathering evidence on Marilyn's murder investigation and then I've been spending the last hour thinking about how I could tell you what I've found."

"We've known each other for twenty years. Just tell me." Adam rubbed the back of his neck as if he was stalling for time. "Well?" I said, trying to prompt him.

"First of all, Marilyn died shortly after nine o'clock, not ten o'clock. It turns out the radio show was not live."

"Yeah, I know. The sheriff told me."

"That clears Hal. He was with seven other cyclists around nine o'clock."

"So," I said with a heavy sigh. "We're back to square one."

"Not square one," Adam said, shaking his head. "Not after what I found out this afternoon."

"And what was that?"

"The sheriff wanted me to research the phone call Marilyn received while she was on the air. We figured it was on her cell phone. We wanted to know who called her and see if they left a message."

"Yeah. What did you find?"

"Nothing," Adam said. "Absolutely nothing."

I stared at Adam for a moment with a puzzled look. "Excuse me?"

He reached into his pocket and pulled out a cell phone. "This is Marilyn's. It shows no record of receiving a call at 9:05."

"That's impossible," I said, reaching over to grab the phone away from him. I began playing with the phone. "Maybe someone deleted it from her cell phone history. I think there is a way to do that."

"I thought of that. That's why I went back to her cell phone company. They show no record of any call coming in at that time either." He handed me a report on the phone company's letterhead and I read it over.

"Let me ask you this," I said, looking back at him. "You did a search of the house. Did you uncover any other cell phone in the house?"

"No."

"So it has to be hers. Look, I'll prove it to you." I got up to grab the CD of the phone call. I set up the CD to the point of the other phone call. "Okay, listen to this." I punched several buttons on her cell phone to initiate ringing. "See, it sounds exactly like the ring on the radio. I know my wife's cell phone ring."

Adam looked down at the floor as there was an eerie silence in the room. He slowly looked back up at me with a cold, piercing glare. "Don't make this harder than it needs to be." He pulled out his gun and my heart rate quickened. "I want you to shut up and just listen, okay."

I couldn't believe what was happening. My friend was turning psycho right in front of me. "Yeah, sure," I said, not wanting to agitate him further.

He slowly reached into his pocket with his free hand. "This is my cell phone. It has an outgoing call at 9:05. Do you know who I called?" I slowly shook my head. "You, but you didn't answer. It just rang and rang."

"I told you. I left my cell phone in the car while I was getting gas."

"Nah," Adam said, shaking his head. "That's a lie. You have the same cell phone as your wife. So, your cell phone ring will match the one on the tape too. More important than that, I synchronized the time on the radio station and my cell phone. The time of the calls matches to the minute."

"Okay, so maybe I left my cell phone back at my house. It rang while she was on the air. So, what?"

"That cell phone was in the kitchen with your wife at 9:05, moments before her death," Adam said, pointing the gun at me. "But, it was with you a mere fifteen minutes later when you arrived at my house. You were making calls from the car, remember? That means you had to come back to retrieve it about the time Marilyn was murdered."

"I didn't come back to the house. And do you mind not pointing that at me?"

"Not until you tell me the truth. Of course you came back. Now, tell me what really happened. Tell me it wasn't premeditated. Tell me you just snapped. But, don't lie. You lie

94

to me and I'll turn all this evidence over to Sheriff Reid and let her deal with it. So, you can deal with her or me. It's your choice."

I rubbed my face as I considered my options. "I didn't mean for it to happen," I finally said, telling the truth. "I was driving over to your house and realized that I had left my cell phone back at the house. I turned around and headed back. I opened the front door and heard my wife talking on the phone, admitting she had an affair. I just snapped, I swear." I dropped my head in shame.

Before I knew it, Adam had snapped handcuffs on my wrists. "I'm taking you into the station."

"Hey, I told you the truth and you're still arresting me?"

"You're my best friend. We're so close I never seriously considered you a suspect," Adam said. "I promised you that the person who killed Marilyn will pay for what they did. I don't break promises, especially to my best friend."

Corner of the Living Room

I looked at Evan from across the room with hate in my eyes. Some people don't deserve to live and Evan is one of those people. A pretty boy in his mid 20s who thinks he's God's gift to women, Evan manipulated younger women with mind games and assaulted them to establish his dominance.

What angered me the most was what he did to Catherine, a sweet, innocent twenty year old who had fallen madly in love with him. Well, the police found Catherine's badly beaten body in a ditch last week. Everyone in town except the police were convinced Evan was responsible. But, it wasn't just Catherine. I had seen his act to other women all too many times. Finally, I would be able to witness an end to his terror and an end to him.

I cracked a smile at the sight of Evan completely helpless in the corner of the living room of my apartment. It was Judgment Day for Evan and I wouldn't have missed this for the world. He had been tied up earlier. His feet were bound with a thick chain at the ankles, and his hands were tied tightly at the wrists with a rope. To be sure that he would not escape, his right leg was chained to the wall. Because of his loud screams for help as he was bound, he had to be gagged. Realizing the gag was too powerful, Evan had given up the struggle to make noise. I looked at my watch. It was 2:40 in the afternoon. There were only twenty minutes left.

"You're about to get yours," I said, hoping my statement would be correct. I glared into Evan's evil eyes as I put my foot up on the coffee table and sunk farther into the couch. Evan frantically banged his head on the wall behind him as he struggled to get free.

"There's no way you're getting out of that," I said with a snicker. I couldn't take my eyes off him. I liked seeing him vulnerable, like all of his female victims had been. It was such poetic justice.

I watched calmly as he actually made progress in freeing his right hand as music played in the background. Then, it happened. He had loosened the bond. His right hand was free!

At that moment, my doorbell rang. "Damn it!" I said in frustration. Right now, I didn't want to get the door. I decided to ignore it. I was more concerned about Evan.

With his right hand free, he quickly pulled the gag out of his mouth and started screaming, "Help! I've been kidnapped! Help! I've been tied up!"

The doorbell rang again. This time followed by the words, "Open the door! This is the police!"

I acted quickly, reaching for an instrument on the coffee table. I pointed it at Evan. Within a split second, he was silenced.

I jogged out of the living room toward the front door. I looked through the peephole and saw two police officers. The larger officer had his right hand on his holstered gun.

I slowly opened the door. "May I help you?"

"I'm Officer Stevens ma'am," the smaller officer said, touching the bill of his hat. He had a mustache and curly black hair, which seemed to be rapidly growing out from underneath his blue police hat. "Sorry to bother you, but we had a complaint that you may have a hostage in there. The neighbors heard some noise."

"Hostage? I don't have a hostage. Who complained?"

"We can't say ma'am. You wouldn't mind if we have a look around, would you?"

"Actually, I do. I'm kind of in the middle of something."

Officer Stevens flashed a facial expression as if he tasted something bitter. "It'll be a lot easier to have us take a quick look around. We can clear this up in just a few minutes."

"When you have a warrant, you can come in. Okay? Have a good day," I said before closing the door. I looked in the peephole. The two officers looked at each for a moment, shrugged, and walked away.

I rushed back to the living room. Evan had freed both of his hands. He had a large, sharp knife in his right hand. Sitting Indian style, he was using the knife to try to cut through the metal chain that was attached to his ankle.

I squinted toward Evan. "Where did you get that knife?" I sat back down on the sofa and stared at him. "You're not getting out of there, so why are you even trying?"

At that moment, my cell phone rang. I groaned with another interruption. When I looked at the caller ID, I recognized that it was my close friend Monica. I picked it up, but kept my eyes peeled on Evan. "Hi Monica."

"Hi, I'm at work. I want an update on Evan. What's happening?"

I looked to the corner of the living room. "He's still chained up, but he's been trying to escape. He's got his hands free and he's been trying to cut his ankle chains with a knife."

"With a knife? Where did he get a knife?"

"I don't know."

"You don't know? Weren't you watching?"

"Well, the police came to my door. Someone reported that I had a hostage in here."

"What? A hostage?"

"Yeah," I said. "My bet is it's old lady Morgan on the first floor. She probably called the police. She's crazy as a loon."

"Ahhh!!!!" Evan screamed.

"What was that?" Monica asked.

"Oh my gosh! Evan cut himself with the knife." As I talked, Evan continued to scream in pain, although his voice began to drop in volume. "He tried to cut his ankle chain. The knife must have slipped. It went right into his calf. Oooh, he's bleeding really badly. Must have hit an artery."

Evan frantically took his shirt off and wrapped it around his leg, but the bleeding continued. I loved seeing the fear in his eyes, but what I really enjoyed was watching him suffer. He started to moan on the ground and twist in agony.

"Talk to me," Monica said. "I hear noises. What's going on?"

"I think he's bleeding to death. You know, the best part is that he did it to himself." I looked back at Evan. His twisting and turning had stopped and his head slumped down. It went dark. I looked at my watch. It was 2:58.

"What's happening now?" Monica asked.

"Nothing. It's over."

"Over? Is he dead?"

"I think so, but I can't be sure."

"Okay," Monica said with a sigh. "You know I could hear Evan's screams over the phone and it made me realize something."

"What's that?"

"You do have a hostage in your house. It's Evan."

It took a moment for it to sink in. I chuckled. "Maybe old lady Morgan isn't so crazy after all." I said goodbye to Monica before looking back toward the corner of the living room. I picked up the remote control from the coffee table and hit the off button. Just 23 more hours before my favorite soap opera would come back on and I would know for sure if Evan survived.

Murder is a Deadly Game

Silver-haired David Morrison wiped the sweat from his brow as the glistening morning sun shone down. A coastal breeze periodically provided relief from the intense heat. Hired as a security guard for the day, David manned a small booth at the entrance to the gated estate. Wearing reading glasses down near the end of his nose, sixty-year-old David reviewed his instructions.

His boss told him that the Bidwells requested him. This was odd, since he had never met them before. Apparently a friend of a friend said he was trustworthy. Pursuant to his instructions, he holstered a black revolver at his side. With the amount being paid for this relatively straightforward job, he did not want to make any mistakes. He took a deep breath as a black Lexus pulled up to the gate. With clipboard in hand, he stepped out of the booth to greet the driver.

The window rolled down, revealing a woman in her fifties. "Is this the Bidwell residence?" she asked.

"Yes, it is. Your name, ma'am?"

"Michelle Reed." As David looked down at his chart, the woman paused to admire the huge estate behind the gates. There was a long driveway that split the green lawn and led up to the large house. Michelle had no idea that her new client, Sara Bidwell, was so wealthy. Sara had contacted her a few days ago needing legal help related to a contractor who had done substandard work. Noticing the security guard staring at her, she asked, "Is there a problem?"

"No, no problem," David said, a little embarrassed. "It's just that you look so familiar. Have we met?"

Michelle looked at him for a moment, tilting her head. "No, I don't think we have."

"You sure?"

At that moment, a motorcycle came to a stop alongside her car. Rick Hamilton, a picture of vibrant youth at nineteen years old, hopped off the motorcycle. Rick was enjoying his summer between his freshman and sophomore year of college. He wore blue jeans and a leather jacket. He took off his helmet and said with a big smile, "Would you look at this place? I can't believe it. Larry's parents are loaded!"

"I'll be with you in a minute, after I help this lady," David said to Rick.

Rick looked at Michelle and his jaw dropped. He walked over to her car door, wagging his finger. "I know you from somewhere."

"No," she slowly said. "We've never met."

"I'm sure we've met," Rick said, bending down to look into the car. "I never forget a face."

"Ma'am, are you some kind of movie star or something?" David asked.

"Hardly," she said with a chuckle. "Now, if you don't mind, I'd like to get inside."

"Yes, of course," David said. Michelle rolled up her window to discourage further conversation. "You," David said, looking at Rick. "Follow me." The two men walked back to the booth. "Weird," David muttered, entering the booth. "We both recognize that woman. She must be famous, but trying to maintain a low profile."

"No, it's not like that. I didn't see her in a movie or on television. I know I have met her. I just can't remember where."

David looked back at the car. Michelle was looking at her watch and then shot a glare toward David. This was enough of a reminder that he had a job to do. "What's your name and who are you here to see?"

After hearing Rick's response, David picked up the phone. A moment passed before he said, "It's David out front. Mrs. Reed is here to see Mrs. Bidwell and there is a Rick Hamilton to see his friend, Larry." After a few seconds, David hung up the phone and hit a button, opening the gates. "You may both drive up to the house where your parties are waiting for you."

At the end of the driveway, a petite woman with sunglasses, heavy makeup, and blond hair was waiting for the two guests. A large, black Doberman Pincher sat obediently at her side. As Michelle brought her car to a halt, the woman walked up to her. "I'm Sara Bidwell, thank you so much for coming."

"Michelle Reed," Michelle said, shaking Sara's hand. "It's nice to meet you in person."

"And you must be Rick," Sara said as Rick got off his motorcycle.

"In the flesh," the young man said with a smile. "Hey, I love dogs. What's his name?"

"Caesar, but it's best not to touch him," Sara said, stepping in between him and the dog. "He's a trained guard dog. Let's all go inside."

The three walked into the house and into the living room, which had a large buffet of breakfast items and juices on the table. Sara turned toward Michelle and said, "My husband is on an important business call. He'll be off soon. In the meantime, help yourself to something to eat or drink while we wait."

"Thank you," Michelle said, putting down her briefcase and pouring herself some orange juice.

"And Larry just got out of the shower," Sara said to Rick. "Please, help yourself to the buffet."

"This place is amazing," Rick said, looking like a kid in the candy store. "But, Larry is on financial aid. How is that possible if you live in a place like this?"

The phone rang. "Hold that thought," Sara said before walking over to the counter to pick it up. "Hello."

"It's David out front. We have a Tony Martinez to see Mr. Bidwell."

"Yes. Please let him in."

"Since that's our last guest to arrive, please accompany Mr. Martinez and escort him into the living room." Sara hung up the phone and walked back over to the buffet table and near her guests.

"I'm telling you," Rick said to Michelle. "I know we've met. I just can't figure out where. Your face is so familiar."

"Maybe we met in a past life," Michelle said, becoming annoyed with Rick's fixation."

Sara wanted to change the topic of conversation. "Rick, how do you know our son?"

"We met in the dorms at college this past year. He emailed me and invited me over here today."

"Well, while we wait for the others in my family," Sara said. "I can show you two the backyard and the view." Sara led the two guests out the sliding glass door. Caesar, who had yet to leave her owner's side, walked outside with them.

The backyard had a panoramic view of the Pacific Ocean. With the house perched on top of a steep cliff, the crashing of the waves could be heard below. As they continued to walk toward the sound of the water, the concrete patio gave way to green grass until they reached a fence. It was a short fence, only about waist high so the view would not be obstructed.

"Can I hop over the fence and have a look?" Rick asked.

"Not a good idea," Sara said, shaking her head. "There is a sheer drop of about 200 feet. It's pretty dangerous."

Detective Tony Martinez, a twenty year veteran in the homicide division, brought his car to a halt at the end of the driveway. During his time off, Tony worked with troubled teens in the community and had been contacted by Andrew Bidwell about his son. Apparently, Larry had fallen into the wrong crowd and Andrew had asked him to visit his son this morning. Tony, a muscular man, looked especially well-built next to David, who was less defined and fifteen years his senior.

Tony and David got out of the car and David said, "Mr. Bidwell is waiting for you in the living room. I'll lead you there."

The two entered the house and walked down the hallway into the living room.

"You must be Tony," Sara said, greeting him with a handshake. "I'm Sara Bidwell. Thank you so much for coming over. My husband will be down in a moment."

"Oh my gosh. Tony Martinez? It's Michelle, Michelle Reed."

"Michelle, what are you doing here? I haven't seen you for what, two years, since you left the D.A.'s office," Tony said. "What are you doing now?"

"I have my own practice. How about you? Still with the department?"

"Yes."

Rick snapped his fingers. "That's it. You're that lawyer. That's where I remember you." Rick jumped up and walked across the room. "I knew I had met you before. I never forget a face."

"Are you Larry?" Tony asked.

"No, no. I'm Rick…" Rick paused a moment as he noticed Tony for the first time. "You were my dad's partner. You're a cop."

"Ricky Hamilton?" Tony said in shock. "Michelle and I spent weeks with you on your testimony."

"I go by Rick now," he said with a smile.

"What an unbelievable coincidence," Michelle said. "The three of us meeting like this."

"Wow, how long has it been?" Tony asked.

"I was nine years old back then," Rick said. "So, it's been about ten years."

David, standing in the corner, asked, "How do you three know each other?"

"Ten years ago, we all worked together to put a man behind bars for life," Michelle said. "A very evil man."

"Scum of the earth is more like it," Rick said.

"What did this guy do?" David asked, his interest piqued.

"He broke into a house and killed a cop," Michelle replied. "Shot him twice in the back."

David paused for a moment as a series of thoughts flashed through his mind. "The last name of this guy wasn't Rivera?"

"Yeah, Carlos Rivera," Tony said. "You heard of him?"

"Yeah, I was the jury foreman in his case."

"Hold on a minute," Michelle said. "You were on the jury that convicted Carlos Rivera?" David nodded his head.

"Everyone get their hands in the air!" a man shouted, pointing a silver pistol at the group. The four stood there motionless, unable to believe their own eyes. They all recognized the gun-wielding man. It was Carlos Rivera.

With Carlos holding a gun, Sara searched the other four. Starting with David, she took his black revolver and deposited it in a cabinet. No one else had any weapons. She locked the cabinet and put the key in her pocket.

"Good," Carlos said to Sara, "Now, put the handcuffs on them."

"Is that really necessary?" Sara asked.

"Yes! There's four of them and only two of us. Now, do it!" Carlos apparently did not count the loyal Caesar, who now sat attentively next to Sara. The clean-shaven Carlos, who was in his mid forties, wore blue slacks and a white polo shirt. His demeanor showed a man who was bubbling over with rage. Everyone wondered if the slightest thing might trigger violence.

As she handcuffed each person's wrists together, she whispered, "Just do everything he asks and he won't hurt you."

Carlos ordered them to all take a seat. Standing up, Carlos towered over everyone else. Holding his pistol, he announced, "There's no Mr. and Mrs. Bidwell, and there's no son, Larry. I'm Carlos Rivera and this is my wife, Sara." Carlos looked at his wife. "You can take off those glasses and that hideous blond wig now."

Sara took off the short blond wig to reveal her natural black hair as Michelle and Tony let out a small gasp as they recognized Carlos' wife.

Carlos walked over to the large chessboard. "I love games. Do you know the key to winning any game? Anyone?" There was silence in the room. "It's staying one step ahead of your opponent."

"You should take up a new hobby," said Michelle, the first hostage to speak. "Murder is a deadly game."

"I didn't murder anyone. In fact, I have never committed a crime in my life."

"You murdered my father," Rick said, looking serious and intense for the first time today. Carlos simply shook his head.

"How are you out of prison?" Michelle asked. "You got a life sentence."

"I escaped, yesterday."

Tony snickered, "You mentioned you haven't committed any crime, but breaking out of prison is a crime."

"Not if I shouldn't have been there in the first place. Each of you had a hand in sending an innocent man to prison."

"The last time I checked, kidnapping is a crime," David said. "Holding people in handcuffs at gunpoint is a crime."

"Look, I apologize about the gun and the handcuffs. If you follow my orders, everyone will be out of here in the next hour, completely unharmed. Do we have an understanding?"

The four hostages looked at each other before nodding.

"Okay, we'll start by putting all our cards on the table," Carlos said. "You can say whatever you want. I'll let you guys start." With the pistol still in his hand, Carlos sat down on his throne-like chair. "Let the games begin."

Everyone looked at each other. No one wanted to speak first. "There's not much to say," Michelle said, breaking the silence. "You're a drug dealer and a cop-killer."

"First of all, I'm not a drug dealer," Carlos said. "Rick's daddy led a search of my house just two days before he was murdered. He didn't find any drugs."

"But, he found something and that's why you went to his house," Michelle said.

"No. I never went to his house and I'm not a drug dealer."

"We can debate all day whether you deal drugs," Michelle said. "But, there's no debate on this. You murdered Paul Hamilton. Your hair fibers were found in the victim's home and traces of his blood were on your jacket in your home. Ballistics showed the bullets dug out of Paul's chest came from your gun retrieved from your house. Plus, an eye witness said he saw you commit the murder."

"That's right. I saw you," Rick said. "Because of you, I grew up without a father. You're evil."

"You shot him in the back," Tony said with disgust. "You're such a coward."

"Hey!" Carlos shouted. "I said you can say anything, but it has to be the truth. You're calling me an evil coward. You guys don't know me."

"I know you," Tony said, glaring at Carlos. I've known you since you were a little punk. You were always getting into trouble."

"You never have gotten over it, have you?"

"Over what?" Tony asked.

"That I'm more successful than you," Carlos said. "Tony and I grew up in the same neighborhood. Everyone thought that he would beat the odds, make it out of our poor neighborhood and be really successful. And they thought that I would be a loser, make nothing out of my life. But, I'm the one that got rich. I'm the success story. You've always been jealous."

Tony sighed. "I'm not jealous of you."

Carlos paused a moment before asking the group, "Come on, what else makes you think I killed this cop? I want to hear."

"Well, the police caught you with a suitcase full of money at the airport, bound for a flight out of the country," David said. "We talked about that in the jury. If you were innocent, you wouldn't have run."

"What can I say? I panicked," Carlos said. "Okay, anything else from anyone?" The room was silent. "Alright, I heard what you guys think I did. Now, it's my turn to talk about what *you* four did. Every man should have the opportunity to confront his accusers." Carlos stood up. "Has anyone seen a perfectly run relay race? You have four people, working together, to complete the task." Carlos gestured to Tony as he said, "We have the corrupt cop on the first leg, planting evidence. You and the victim were pretty close, right?"

"We were partners," Tony said sternly.

"Yeah, partners, part of the police brotherhood. He has your back. You have his. Hey, why didn't you have his back that night? Where were you?" Carlos asked, pointing at Tony.

"We were off duty. I was at home. I didn't..."

"That's right. You weren't there. And since everyone knows you weren't there for your partner, you wanted to save face by making sure someone paid for this crime. So you set me up."

Tony shook his head. "I didn't."

"Sure you did. Then you passed the baton to a nine year-old kid." Carlos walked over to Rick. "And you took that baton and ran with it, didn't you junior?" Rick remained quiet, his characteristic smile had long sense disappeared. Carlos looked at Rick. "I want you to say the words 'I don't know'." A few seconds passed. "Say it!" Carlos shouted, raising his gun and pointing it at Rick's head.

"I don't know," Rick said, glaring at Carlos with hate in his eyes.

"Say, I'm not sure."

"I'm not sure," Rick responded, this time without prompting.

"See, was that so hard?" Carlos said mockingly before dropping the gun to his side. "But no, you make up this ridiculous story about me breaking into your house at night and murdering your father. You said that someone killed your father at around 9:00?"

"Not someone, you," Rick said bravely. "I remember seeing you wearing a baseball cap and a black jacket. The same jacket where they later found traces of my father's blood."

Carlos bent down coming eye to eye with the seated Rick. "Sara!" Carlos shouted, but keeping his eyes trained on Rick. "Where was I the night that Rick's father was killed?"

"Like I said in court, you were with me, all night."

"You heard her, Rick," Carlos said. "I was with her the whole night. I can't be in two places at once. So, how could I have been at your house killing your father? Huh, huh?" Rick glared back at Carlos, but did not speak. "It was nighttime. You testified that there was only one hallway light on where your father was shot. You said the killer wore a baseball cap. You must have some doubts about what you really saw?"

Rick's eyes closed slightly. "There's no doubt about what I saw. My dad let you in and you closed the front door and then you shot him twice in the back. You even checked his body to make sure he was dead. I saw it all from behind the living room chair."

Carlos straightened up and began pacing when he said, "That's right. You were all the way down the hallway in the living room."

"I know what I saw. I never forget a face. I'm sure it was you."

"You were nine years old!" Carlos exclaimed. "You were sure there was a Santa Claus." Carlos turned his attention to Michelle. "So, Rick here passed the baton to you in the courtroom. I have never seen such a despicable performance in my life. You twisted the facts and suppressed evidence. You never should have tried the case. You should have recused yourself since you have a relationship with the victim."

"A business relationship. I was in the prosecutor's office and he worked homicide."

"No, I had a private investigator look into it. You two had a personal relationship."

"We had a friendship," Michelle said. "But, it was purely platonic."

"Of course, because he was married with a young son. So, we have a corrupt cop, lying eyewitness, and unethical prosecutor. Still, they never would have completed the race without you, the anchorman," Carlos said, pointing at David. "You were the head juror. All you had to say was two simple words, 'not guilty'."

111

"Look," David said. "I decided based on the evidence given to me."

"Cut the crap," Carlos said. "I was there, remember. You deliberated for two hours. You couldn't have come to a just decision in only two hours. All you cared about was getting out of there."

"So, it's a big conspiracy," Michelle said. "We all conspired to get you. Do you know how ridiculous that is?"

"Shut up," Carlos said. "New rule. No one talks unless I ask a question. In fact, talk time is over. It's time for action. Sara, pass them out." Sara walked over to a nearby drawer and pulled out a small stack of papers. She walked back over to the group. "Okay, Sara is passing out sworn statements. Take your time and read it. Tony, yours says you tampered with evidence. Rick, yours says you were not sure of what you saw that night. Michelle, yours says you violated several ethical rules that are grounds for a re-trial and David, I like yours most of all. It says that you believe that I am not guilty." Everyone took the next couple of minutes to read their statement while Sara dropped off pens in front of them.

"Okay, times up," Carlos said. "Everyone sign the statements." Everyone except Tony signed immediately.

"This is bull. I'm not signing this."

"Are you crazy? Just do it," David muttered.

"No."

Carlos pulled out his pistol and put it within inches of Tony's forehead. "Sign it or I'll blow your head off."

Tony slowly picked up the pen and scribbling his signature.

"Good, now the video," Carlos said. "Sara is going to videotape each of you reading from these cue cards." Sara set up the camera and everyone read over their cue cards. "Okay, we'll have the corrupt cop go first. Sit in the chair."

Tony slowly walked over to the chair. Carlos quickened his pace by shoving him toward the chair.

Sara focused the camera to film his chest and up. "This is bogus," Tony said as he realized what the cue cards' message said.

"Just read the cards," Carlos said, losing patience. He motioned to Sara to begin filming."

"Hi, my name is Tony Martinez. I was the lead investigator in Paul Hamilton's murder." As Tony read from the cue cards, it was obvious his heart was not behind his spoken words. "I am of sound mind and not being coerced in any way, when I say that I... uh, I, um..., I did absolutely nothing wrong and Carlos Rivera was properly convicted of this crime which..."

"Cut, cut, cut!" Carlos said, burying his face in his hand. "Alright, now you think this is some kind of a game." Carlos handed Sara his pistol before taking off his shirt. Bare chested, it was clear that Carlos had been working out regularly during his incarceration. "Okay. Let's go," Carlos said, lifting his fists in a boxing stance.

Still seated, Tony lifted his handcuffed hands in the air. "You want me to fight when I have these on?"

"Yeah."

"No!" Sara said upset. "That's not why we're here. Put your shirt back on." Sara handed Carlos his shirt and he reluctantly took it. It was surprising to see Sara hold some power over her husband.

As Carlos put his shirt back on, Michelle asked, "May I have a private word with Tony? It'll be just one minute."

"Be my guest," Carlos said. "But, you both stay in here."

"Michelle walked over to Tony and whispered, "Do the stupid video! You know as well as I do that it is not admissible. We have four eye witnesses that we did it under duress."

"I know that," Tony whispered back. "But, what if this video makes it back to the media? I don't want one person to doubt my integrity. I spent my life building up a reputation. I will not throw that away for nothing."

"For nothing? It will help us can get out of here," Michelle argued.

"Come on, he's not going to let us go. He's a murderer, remember. After we jump through his stupid hoops, he's going to kill all of us." Michelle's eyes widened with the realization.

"Okay, counsel time is over," Carlos said, clapping his hands. "Are you going to do the video correctly?"

"Tell you what," Tony said. "You release Michelle right now and I'll do the video just as you wrote it. But, you have to release her first. You'll still have three hostages."

"No," Carlos said, shaking his head. "You don't make the rules. I do. I said I'll release everyone, but it'll happen when I'm ready." Carlos pointed his pistol at Tony. "So, are you going to do the video?"

Tony looked at Michelle and then back at Carlos, "No."

"Damn it!" Carlos said, his face a crimson red. He took the pistol back from Sara. "Fine! Tony, you're responsible for everything that happens next. Everyone, go the backyard, now!"

Carlos ushered everyone outside on the patio. "Go get David's gun out of the cabinet," he said to his wife. Sara went back inside and returned shortly holding the black revolver. "This should be you, but I need your video," Carlos said to Tony. "David, on the other hand is expendable." Carlos grabbed David's arm and led him onto the grass and toward the fence.

"You hurt him in any way," Tony said. "I swear I'll kill you!"

"You can stop this if you agree to do the video!" Carlos shouted as he continued to escort David toward the cliff. When he got to the fence, Carlos turned back to the group and exclaimed to Sara, "You keep that revolver trained on those three! If any of them so much as takes a step toward me, instruct Caesar to attack. If any one comes toward you, shoot 'em." Sara nodded. Carlos turned to David and said, still holding his pistol, "Step over the fence and then kneel down."

David followed Carlos' directions before begging, "Please don't hurt me. I'll do whatever you want. Say whatever you want."

"Okay, this is your last chance, Tony!" Carlos yelled from the other side of the yard. "If you don't agree to do the video, I am going to put a bullet in this man's head."

"Tony, please!" Michelle pleaded. "Just do what he wants."

Tony rubbed his face as he quickly considered his options. "He's not going to kill him," Tony finally said.

"The hell I won't!" Carlos shouted.

"Damn it man," Rick said. "Just do the video. You can save his life!"

"You're so naïve," Tony said. "If I'm wrong and he kills him because I don't do a stupid video, we're all as good as dead anyway. He'd never let us go. And I'm going out on my own terms."

"I'm losing patience for this!" Carlos said, shouting. "So Tony, you want to play a game. Let's play a game of chicken. On the count of five, I will pull this trigger!"

"Oh mighty God, help me," David said before reciting a prayer as he closed his eyes.

Michelle, giving up on Tony, turned her attention to Sara. "If your husband was really with you when that cop was killed, this is the wrong way to prove he's innocent."

"Okay, this is on your conscience Tony!" Carlos shouted. "One!"

"Stop this, Sara!" Michelle exclaimed.

"Two!" Carlos screamed.

"Don't do it, Carlos!" Sara shouted, still looking at the other three hostages.

"Three!"

"Carlos!" Sara shouted. As she turned toward Carlos, she dropped the gun on the ground.

Tony acted immediately. Even handcuffed, he was able to pick up the gun, pushing aside a slower Sara, who also went for the gun. With the gun in hand, Tony fired at Carlos, hitting him in the chest.

Caesar, reacting to the gunfire and seeing Sara knocked down, attacked Tony. Leaping through the air, the Doberman knocked him down.

Meanwhile, blood spilled from Carlos' chest. He had a look of disbelief. He instinctively dropped his pistol and pressed both hands against his blood-drenched shirt. His eyes widened as he staggered backwards. Losing his footing, he screamed as he fell off the cliff.

"Help!" a grounded Tony screamed as the Doberman attacked his left arm. David, stunned momentarily that he was still alive, hopped over the small fence and back toward the house to try to aid Tony. Handcuffed, Rick and Michelle were limited, but used their feet to try to kick the Doberman off of him. The dog remained focused on who he viewed as the attacker and sunk his teeth into Tony's left forearm. Tony shrieked in pain.

With everyone else preoccupied, Sara was able to pick up the revolver, which was on the ground. "Heel Caesar, heel!" she shouted as she pointed the gun at the other three.

Caesar abruptly ended his attack and walked to Sara's side. David and Rick tended to the injured Tony while Michelle appealed to Sara. "Please, give me the gun. It's over."

"I can't do that," Sara said, shaking her head. "He killed my husband."

"Yes, you can," Michelle said. She looked at Tony who was moaning in pain on the ground. "He needs medical attention urgently. Give me the gun."

Tony winced in pain. "Give her the gun and I'll make sure that you don't do any jail time for all of this."

"Why should I trust you?" Sara asked.

Tony gritted his teeth as he said, "Because you have my word. And my word is always good." Sara slowly handed Michelle the gun.

Michelle muttered to David, "Game over."

Everyone was taken down to the police station for questioning. Tony had initially spent time with a doctor, treating multiple dog bites on his left forearm. Now, he was being questioned by Lt. Carolyn Myers. Carolyn, Tony's boss, headed the homicide division. A fervent believer in justice, Carolyn poured her heart and soul into her job. Affectionately known as "bulldog" for her devotion and perseverance, she had a gift to be amazingly compassionate with victims and ruthlessly tough on suspects. But when she talked to her longtime colleague Tony, she treated him as a friend.

"So, I hear you were quite the hero today," Carolyn said. Tony's smile gave way to a slight grimace as he sat down. His movements had aggravated the pain of his injuries. "So, how's the arm?"

"I'll live," Tony said, shifting in his chair. "Did anyone tell you how we got Sara to surrender?"

Carolyn flashed a puzzled look. "No, not yet."

"I promised her that she wouldn't do any jail time."

"And that did the trick?" Carolyn asked. Tony nodded. Carolyn wagged her finger. "Nice thinking." Carolyn began looking at an open file.

"Believe it or not. I want to keep my word."

Carolyn suddenly stopped reading her file and looked up at Tony in disbelief. "You despised the Riveras. You would have been the last person that I would expect to come to Sara's defense. Even if you made a promise."

"It's not about the promise, it's about what's right. Don't get me wrong. I hate this woman. I really do. She committed perjury ten years ago. She helped Carlos escape from prison. She engaged in fraud to lure us to the house. But, once I took my emotions out of it, I realized there was really only one bad guy here and his body is somewhere in the Pacific Ocean. Arresting Sara just isn't necessary."

"Wow, a hero who is compassionate and forgiving. I'll note your argument against arresting Sara, but that's for the D.A. to decide. Now, you need to take a step back from this case."

"Alright," Tony said nodding.

After hours of debriefing and questions from the police, Michelle recognized a very familiar face. It was the district attorney, the distinguished Kenneth L. Hoover. Michelle, who had worked for him during her last two years as a prosecuting attorney, knew him as simply, "Ken". Dressed in a suit and tie, Ken was a no-nonsense type a guy. Although tough to work for at times, you would want him working on the people's case if you lost a loved one to homicide. Bright and cunning, he always kept a calm and composed exterior, no matter what chaos was going on around him.

Ken had over twenty-five years of experience working for the prosecution, but he was a relative newcomer to this county. His reputation, as well as the department's, meant everything to him.

"You know how I hate to come in the office on the weekends," Ken lamented. "But when I heard what happened, I wanted to come down for myself and follow the police investigation from the beginning. This time, I don't want any mistakes."

Michelle dipped her head. "I hope you aren't implying that mistakes were made ten years ago."

Ken smiled. "I wouldn't know. I wasn't around back then. I just want to make sure there are no mistakes now, okay?" Michelle nodded and Ken continued, "I'm going to be exploring every angle of this case to make sure the department doesn't look foolish."

"Well I've told the police everything that happened. Have they uncovered anything of note in their investigation?"

"It's not what they found, it's what they haven't found. Despite scouring the water near the home, they haven't found Carlos Rivera's body."

Michelle raised her eyebrows. "Really," she said, pausing to think. "The current could have carried it anywhere."

"Yep, suppose that's possible," Ken said, scratching his head. "Not having a body though, that makes me nervous. I mean, how do we know that Carlos is really dead?"

"Oh, he's dead, I assure you."

Ken leaned forward. "How do you know for sure? A man could survive a fall from that cliff."

"Maybe, just maybe, he could survive the fall," Michelle conceded. "One of the policemen said the tide was high, so the ocean was very deep by the cliff. So maybe he could have swum to safety, but not after he was shot in the chest. Did you see a blood trail anywhere along the waters' edge?"

Ken stared at her for a few moments. "Well no, but we don't know he was really shot."

"Of course we do. I saw Tony fire the gun and Carlos' blood spurt from his chest."

"Maybe he was shot with blanks and Carlos had some kind of blood pack on him."

"No," Michelle said firmly. "He was shot with David's revolver and he confirmed it was loaded with real bullets."

Ken jotted down some notes on his pad before asking, "Could Carlos have been wearing a bullet proof vest of some kind?"

"No, he even took his shirt off to fight Tony at one point. He was completely bare chested. And he never left our sight after that."

Ken, deep in thought, began tapping the head of his pencil on his desk. "There's something else that's bothering me. Suppose that Carlos Rivera did not kill Paul Hamilton ten years ago."

"That's not possible. We have blood evidence, ballistics, an eye-witness."

"Hold on," Ken said. "I'm asking you to take it as a given. Just for the next five minutes. Assume that Carlos did not kill Paul. Agreed?"

"Agreed," Michelle said with a sigh.

"With that assumption, Carlos Rivera spent ten years in jail wrongly. An innocent man in jail for ten years."

"That would be a travesty, but that's still no excuse for what he did to us."

"What did he really do? Did he beat anybody up? Did he rape anybody? Did he kill anybody?"

"Well no. But, that's only because Tony stopped him. He was going to kill David."

"Do you really know that?" Ken asked. "Maybe all he wanted to do was scare you guys into doing this video and signing the statement to prove his innocence."

"He wasn't innocent. He killed Paul Hamilton."

"Ah, ah, ah, ah. We agreed to assume he didn't do that," Ken said, which prompted another heavy sigh from Michelle. "So under the assumption that he was not a murderer before that day, is it possible that he didn't become one all of a sudden? Perhaps he was simply trying to scare Tony into complying to do the video."

"No, not possible."

"Really, why not?"

"Look, you weren't there. I was. Carlos was upset and frustrated. He had his pistol up to David's head and he was going to shoot the man who under your assumption had wrongly found him guilty and stole ten years of his life."

"Did Carlos shoot anyone else with his pistol earlier?"

"No, but so what? He was going to shoot David. I'm sure of it."

"As sure as you are that Carlos killed Paul Hamilton?"

"Yes."

Ken tossed a file in front of Michelle. "The highlighted section. Read it."

Her forehead wrinkled as she picked up the file. A moment later, she fell back in her chair. The police report stated that they retrieved Carlos' silver pistol. There were no bullets in it. She stared at the police report in disbelief.

Ken said, "I had an opportunity to read the statements that Carlos had wanted all of you to sign. Any possibility there's truth in them?"

Michelle, still stunned by the information in the police report, slowly looked up at Ken. "No," she said, snapping out of her trance.

"Nothing about your conduct during the court proceeding could be considered questionable?"

She looked at Ken for a moment, annoyed he would even ask such a question. "No, Carlos' legal team has been trying to get a re-trial for the last ten years. They have failed because I did nothing wrong. Nothing."

"What about Tony? Any possibility that he could have planted some of the damning evidence."

"No. He's well respected in the department. He would never do anything like that."

"I'm not asking for a character assessment. I'm asking if he had the opportunity."

"He was one of the first officers to arrive at Carlos' house. He was a part of the team that uncovered Carlos' blood stained jacket." Ken raised his eyebrows. "But," Michelle said, raising her index finger in the air. "Tony never went to the crime scene. He never had an opportunity to plant Carlos' hair on the victim's body."

Ken thought for a moment. "What about Rick? Any chance he was lying or mistaken about seeing Carlos? He was just a kid."

"A kid who was consistent in saying what he saw. We had a child psychologist interview him. Tony, who is really good with kids, spent a lot of time with him. They both agreed. Rick was telling the truth."

Ken began thumbing through some paperwork. "And David, Carlos thinks he…"

"What is it with you? How can you believe that there's some conspiracy to get Carlos? What? Just because he held us hostage with a bullet-less gun."

"I'm only asking questions. I've drawn no conclusions. You can't draw an appropriate conclusion until you have asked all of the questions."

"I know that you're just doing your job, but here's the thing. You never knew Paul Hamilton."

"No," Ken said slowly. "But that has nothing to do with what I'm trying…"

"It has everything to do with it!" Michelle snapped. "Paul was a great cop: fair, honest, and hard working. He always did the right thing. Most of your current police department knew his character and loved him for it. And those guys all believe that we have Paul's killer in custody. So, just be careful who you ask your questions to. You can become a real unpopular guy around here."

In a nearby holding room, David and Rick sat, waiting. They had each been interviewed by the police and were now wondering what would happen next. Quietly, each were thinking about their emotional and adrenaline packed day.

Finally David spoke. "Makes you wonder. The guy escapes from prison, but then goes through all this trouble to get us together. I mean, why didn't he just flee to the North Pole where no one would find him?"

"Cuz he's nuts," Rick replied. "He was a psycho killer. Who knows and who cares?"

David bit his lower lip as he told himself that he needed to tread lightly with Rick when discussing anything related to Carlos. "Well, I'm just glad it's over," David said diplomatically. "I never want to think about Carlos Rivera again."

"There hasn't been a day in the last ten years that I haven't thought about him. The guy's in my nightmares and consumes my thoughts during the day."

"But now, he's fish food on the bottom of the ocean," David said. "Maybe that can bring you some peace." Rick nodded as he thought about David's words. Just then, the door to the holding room was opened and an officer escorted Tony into the room.

"What's going on?" Rick asked Tony as the officer left. "When are they going to let us go home?"

"They've already debriefed us individually. They should let us go soon. Michelle is meeting with the D.A. now. He might want to question us as well."

"I hate police stations, the endless questions, the long waiting," Rick said. "This reminds me so much of when my father was murdered."

"Hang in there. We'll be done soon," Tony said, giving Rick a big hug. Tony's presence made things a lot easier for him. An emotional Rick wiped away a tear after the two ended their embrace.

"I just want to thank you, again," David said, extending his hand to Tony. "You saved my life today. You're a hero."

"You're welcome, again," Tony said smiling as he shook David's hand. "But, I'm no hero."

"Are you kidding? You saved all of our lives," Rick said. "Who knows what that lunatic would have done."

"Sorry to keep you all here at the station so long," Ken said, entering the room with Michelle right behind him. "My name is Kenneth Hoover. I'm the D.A. I appreciate your patience. You are all free to leave." Rick immediately reached for his jacket while David started for the door.

"Are you going to arrest Sara?" Tony asked, which stopped all movement in the room.

All eyes were on Ken. "No, not at this time."

"What?" Rick said. "She held us hostage. How can you just let her go?"

"It's probably for the best," Tony said. "No arrest means we won't have to re-live this whole ordeal in yet another court case."

"It still sucks," Rick said. "She just gets away with what she did."

"No one is getting away with anything, I promise," Ken said. "When we have enough evidence to convict someone of a crime, we'll make an arrest." Ken patted Rick on the shoulder and led the four out of the room.

After the four had left the police station, Ken walked over to a nearby holding room where Sara and her attorney were waiting. "Okay, we're done with our questions, for now. You are free to leave, but please notify us if you will be leaving the area."

"My husband was innocent," Sara said, rising. "He was with me when that cop was shot ten years ago. Today, he was just trying to prove his innocence. He was wrongly accused, convicted, and now executed by the police. Where's the justice in that?"

"I'm sorry you lost your husband today Mrs. Rivera," Ken said. "But, don't look to me for sympathy. He was a convicted murderer who escaped from prison. And once out, you two held four hostages at gunpoint and intended on putting a bullet in an innocent man's head. That is absolutely unforgivable. However, there won't be an arrest until there is a full investigation. Justice will be served, which includes reviewing the original case against your husband."

"That's good," Sara said as she passed Ken in the doorway. "But it's about ten years too late."

Exactly ten days later, Carolyn was back in Ken's office. "We still haven't found Carlos' body in the ocean. There's no record of him or anyone fitting his description being treated at any local hospital. We're calling off the search and officially listing him as "presumed dead".

"That's okay, officially," Ken said. "But in reality, we have to assume he's still alive."

"Given the evidence, that's highly unlikely," Carolyn said, shaking her head.

"Maybe, but it doesn't make sense that Carlos, after escaping from jail, to gather the four people who convicted him for the sole purpose of securing their written statements and video." He leaned back in his chair and looked up at the ceiling for a few moments. "Here's what would make a lot more sense. He got all of the parties together to merely stage his death. What better eyewitnesses to his death than the people who had a hand in his conviction. We know they rented the estate for the week. They specifically chose a place on the edge of a cliff. With Carlos presumed dead, any man hunt for him would be called off."

"To believe Carlos is still alive, there would have to been collusion. At least one person, if not two, would have had to be involved."

"That's right," Ken said. "And you can bet that they'll contact him eventually. We'll make a public statement that we won't be making an arrest in the case."

"We run the risk that we'll lose Sara," Carolyn said. "She might run. Maybe we should cut our losses and arrest Sara on the kidnapping charge. We're sure that she's guilty of that."

"I think Carlos is alive. And if I'm right, Sara will lead us right to him. She can't do that in jail. Besides, Carlos is the one that I want."

"Okay," Carolyn said rising. "You handle the announcement. I'll put a team on Sara's surveillance."

"One more thing. I want the surveillance to be top secret. Only those officers assigned should know. I definitely don't want any of Carlos' hostages, including Tony, to know about this."

"No problem," Carolyn said before leaving.

Four months came and went and Sara's surveillance had yet to uncover anything. No contact with any of the hostages or even anyone who could possibly be Carlos. In fact, the most noteworthy event was what Sara freely admitted to the police. She called Carolyn to inform her that she was selling the house and moving to Lima, Peru to live with relatives. She left a contact number where she could be reached in Peru.

Over the next four days, the police tracked Sara's movements. They booked the same flight into Lima, Peru and once in Lima, trailed her to her relatives' house. Sara stayed in Lima for another two weeks before taking a bus to Cusco, Peru. In Cusco, she stayed in a small condo and rarely left. Once she left the condo with a man with a beard and mustache.

When this information got back to Carolyn, she immediately wondered if this man was in fact Carlos. Photos taken from a distance by the surveillance team were inconclusive.

A few days later, on a Monday, Sara and her male friend went out for breakfast. As soon as they were finished with their meal, a member of the surveillance team swooped in and confiscated the drinking glasses.

By Tuesday morning, the lab results were in. Fingerprints on the glass matched Carlos Rivera's. Carolyn began coordinating with the police in Peru. However, she wanted to oversee the capture of Carlos Rivera personally.

That morning, she lined up two of her best detectives to accompany her to Cusco, Peru.

As she was about to leave for the airport, there was a knock on her office door. It was Tony. "I hear Jones and Sullivan are going to Peru on a special assignment. What's going on?"

"It doesn't relate to your case load," Carolyn said, looking at her computer screen.

"Okay, but it's pretty unusual for us to be flying detectives to South America. What's going on?"

Carolyn turned away from her computer screen and looked at Tony. "I can't talk about this."

"Why? You can't answer a simple question. What's this… Tony stopped in mid sentence. "Wait a minute. Does this have something to do with Carlos Rivera?" Carolyn simply stared at him. "Come on, tell me, please!"

Carolyn paused for a moment. "Close the door." As Tony closed the glass door to the office, she took a couple of items off the top of her desk and stored them in the drawers. Then, she walked around her desk and in front of him. "Come here." After Tony approached her, Carolyn began straightening his blue tie. "Look at you. Your tie is crooked and it's not tight enough." Tony awkwardly looked out the office window to see if anyone was watching them. She then whispered, "You must keep this

between us. If you tell anyone, I swear I'll have your badge."
She started to tighten his tie. "Got it?"

Tony playfully gasped for air. "Yes, what is it?"

She let go of his tie. "Carlos is alive and hiding in South America. We're going to pick him up."

"Wait, hold on a minute. He's alive!"

"Shh!"

"How's that possible?" Tony asked in a much lower tone. "I shot him four months ago. He fell off a cliff."

Carolyn opened her desk drawer and pulled out a file. "We have pictures of a man that Sara has been seeing in South America." She spread the pictures on her desk. "We followed this man to a restaurant. The fingerprints on his drinking glass prove it's Carlos."

Tony staggered back, having to take a seat to avoid falling down. "He's alive?"

"I'm sorry to cut this short, but I have to be at the airport in an hour."

"I want to go with you. Be a part of the team that brings Carlos back."

"Out of the question."

"What? Why? This man killed my partner. He held me hostage and faked his death."

"That's why I can't have you on this case. You're too emotionally involved."

"Look, Jones and Sullivan are good, but you know I'm the department's best detective. You need me."

Carolyn paused as if she was trying to figure out what to do. "Can you leave for the airport in five minutes?" she finally asked.

"Yes."

Carolyn and Tony sat in adjacent seats on their flight down to Peru. Two of their department's top detectives, Jones and Sullivan, were one row in front of them. Tony looked over to a grinning Carolyn. It was a stark contrast to her usual demeanor.

"What are you smiling about?" Tony asked.

"I was just thinking about Paul. He was a good man and a great cop, but boy was he ever stubborn."

"Just like me," Tony said with a chuckle. "That's why we made such good partners."

"Yeah, but what I admired about him is that he always stood up for what was right, no matter what. He believed in justice."

Tony wagged his finger in the air. "And that's why we need to make sure justice is served in Paul's case. We need to get Carlos."

"We will," Carolyn said, reclining her seat slightly. "We will."

After they landed, they drove rented cars to Cusco and to the city's police station. The local police were awaiting their arrival. For about thirty minutes, the U.S. detectives and Peruvian police strategized in a conference room how they would apprehend Carlos. The local police had staked out the house and believed Sara and Carlos were inside. All they needed now was a warrant from the local court, which was due to arrive shortly.

While they were waiting for the warrant, they decided to take a break from their meeting. Carolyn ducked into a side room and called Ken on her cell phone.

"So, you have any news for me?" Carolyn asked.

"No, you'll be happy to hear that he hasn't done anything," Ken said. "At least not yet."

"That means he isn't going to do anything. I told you."

"When are you going to move in on Carlos?"

"We're dealing with some red tape. It will probably happen in the next hour."

"Well, I'm going to continue to monitor," Ken said.

"You go right ahead, but it's a waste of time. I gotta go." Carolyn hung up the phone and returned to the conference room. "Where's Tony?"

"He left to use the restroom," Detective Sullivan replied.

Carolyn shrugged. She sat down and began talking to the local police.

Meanwhile, Tony pulled the rental car over to the side of the dirt road, about three houses away from the targeted address. He got out and walked down the road and up the walkway toward the house. Tony put his ear to the front door. He could hear music. He pulled out his gun and slowly tried the front door. It was unlocked! The music drowned out the sound of the front door opening. Devoid of fear, the experienced detective was focused and determined. He walked toward the music, his gun pointed out at any would-be adversary.

"Freeze!" Tony shouted as he entered the living room. Sara was sitting on the couch and a man was playing pool. "Still playing games, eh Carlos," Tony said, pointing the gun at him. "Game time is over. Put the cue stick down, now!"

"I'm not Carlos," the man said, placing the cue stick on the table and then raising his hands.

"This is my cousin," Sara said. "You might remember. You shot and killed Carlos."

"Forget the song and dance. We've been tracking you for the last few weeks. We have pictures matching your new look. And we took fingerprints off one of your drinking glasses. It confirms that you're Carlos Rivera." The man took a step toward the back hallway. "Alright, you take another step and I will shoot you!" Tony said, pointing the gun toward his head. "And this time, I assure you. There are real bullets in the gun."

"Just leave us alone," the man said.

"Hmm, let's see," Tony said. "You dealt drugs. Murdered an officer. Escaped from prison. Held four hostages. Faked your death. And you think I should just let you go?" Tony glared at Carlos as he looked at his full beard and mustache, a clear attempt to alter his appearance. "You think you're pretty smart. You tricked the four of us to come to your house just to witness your death." Tony looked at Sara. "You dropped the gun on purpose. You knew I would pick it up and fire at Carlos. I've been thinking about it. David loaded the gun with real bullets, but when we were all outside, you went back inside to retrieve the revolver. That's when you replaced the real bullets with blanks."

"Okay, you got me. I staged my death, but I did not kill Paul," Carlos said. "Open your mind for just a minute. Paul was shot in the back. That means it was by someone he knew and trusted. He never would have turned his back on me."

"Paul would have turned his back if you had a gun and ordered him to. Besides, there's tons of physical evidence. Your hair on Paul's body, bullets from your gun, and Paul's blood on your jacket."

"You planted the gun and jacket to frame me."

Tony snickered. "That's your solution for everything. I set you up. Listen closely. It's impossible. I was one of the first officers at your house to arrest you, but I never was at the crime scene." A chill went up Carlos' spine as a stark realization hit him.

Carlos looked at Sara, saying, "No police report records him at the crime scene because he went before Rick called 911, before the police were called." Carlos turned toward Tony and said, "You were there when you killed him. That's why Paul turned to walk down the hall. He trusted you."

"You have some nerve," Tony said. "It was your bloody jacket and your gun that shot him. Rick identified you."

"You must have stolen the gun and jacket from me," Carlos said, before pausing to think. "You were Paul's partner. You were a part of the search of my house two days before the murder. You must have taken them then."

"Rick identified you," Tony said forcefully.

"A nine year old kid can be influenced," Carlos said. "Especially by an officer and family friend who worked with him on his testimony."

"Enough," Tony said, aiming his gun at Carlos with an outstretched hand. "Another word and I blow your brains out right now." Carlos bit his lower lip and remained silent. "I wanted to talk to you about something," Tony said, slowly dropping the gun back to his side. "The day you took me hostage, you said something that has really been bothering me. You said that you are more successful than me because you're rich." Tony shook his head. "Here's a life lesson. You don't measure success by how wealthy you are."

"No?" Carlos said. "Fill me in. What determines success?"

"Reputation. How others view you. I'm a respected officer of the law. You're an escaped convict, hiding out in a foreign country. So, you tell me. Who do you think people consider more successful?" When Carlos didn't answer, Tony tossed him handcuffs. "Put these on your wrists." Tony threw handcuffs to Sara with the same instructions. They each locked the handcuffs to both wrists. "Okay, let's go outside. You first Sara," Tony said, gesturing with his gun. She got up and led them out of the front door and toward a car parked on the street.

"Get in the backseat of the car," Tony said to Sara.

Once Sara had entered the car, Carlos said to Tony, "You're not successful. You're just an idiot. You always have been. I didn't murder your partner. Every day you wake up remember you put an innocent man in jail."

Tony grabbed Carlos and slammed him against the car. He pressed his left arm against his neck and whispered, "You know how you say you like games? How does it feel to get played? Yeah, played. I murdered Paul and framed you for it."

"Why are you telling me this?"

Tony smiled, "Because I can. And that's what makes a great reputation so powerful. Who's going to listen to you? A convicted murderer's word against a decorated cop."

"So that makes you successful?"

"Yeah, it does. Every day for the rest of your life when you wake up in your jail cell, you can thank me for the accommodation."

With Carlos and Sara in the backseat, Tony eyed them in the rear view mirror as he drove to the police station. Once he arrived, he honked the horn repeatedly. A Peruvian police officer and Detective Sullivan were the first to come out. Carolyn followed right behind them.

"Where have you been?" Carolyn asked. "We're about to get the go ahead to pick up Carlos."

"Take a look at the backseat," Tony said. "I've got a present for you."

"What?" Detective Sullivan said. "You picked him up on your own."

Carolyn grabbed Tony by the tie. "I swear. I could choke you for breaking protocol on this one." She pulled him closer. "If you ever pull a stunt like this again, I'm taking your badge. Do you hear me?"

"Loud and clear," Tony replied.

Carolyn let go of Tony and, along with a Peruvian officer, escorted Carlos and Sara into the police station.

Back inside the police station, Tony recounted his story of Carlos' capture to Detective Sullivan, Detective Jones, and the other Peruvian officers.

"Great job," Detective Sullivan said. "The mayor is going to give you the key to the city for bringing Carlos back."

"Just doing my job."

Detective Jones leaned closer to him. "Well, your old partner, Paul, would have been proud. You did right by him, putting Carlos back in jail."

"Sorry to interrupt," Carolyn said, entering the room. "But, we have a debrief to do." The other officer cleared out of the room and Carolyn gestured to Tony to take a seat. Tony sat down. "We're going to do a debrief on Carlos' capture, on the record," Carolyn said, placing a tape recorder on the table. "You know the drill."

"Sure," Tony said. He proceeded to account in simple terms for why he went ahead of the rest of the group to pick up Carlos. He described the apprehension as uneventful. He handcuffed an unarmed man and his wife and then brought them into custody.

"Did you use force?"

"No."

"Did you tell Carlos that you murdered Paul and are framing him for it?"

Tony straightened up in his chair. He tilted his head as he asked, "Is that what Carlos told you?"

"Answer the question, please."

"No," Tony said, folding his arms. "I never told him that."

"Not even out of frustration or as a tactic?"

"No," Tony said forcefully.

"If you had told him that you murdered Paul, would it have been the truth?"

"What's going on? Is this a debrief or an interrogation? You know I didn't murder my partner, my friend, Paul." Tony stared at Carolyn in disbelief. "Now, tell me what this all about. What did Carlos tell you?"

"Absolutely nothing," Carolyn said, reaching into her pocket. "He refused to talk to us without a lawyer." Tony flashed a perplexed look. "Do you know what this is?" Carolyn asked, holding a small object between her thumb and index finger.

Tony squinted. "It looks like some kind of pin."

"It's a bug and I put it on the back of your tie when we were in my office before making the trip."

"What? Why?"

"I did it to placate Ken," Carolyn said. "He thought there was a chance that you were working with Carlos. That you were going to warn him that we were coming."

"That's ridiculous."

"It turns out that it was, but the bug did pick up your entire conversation with the Riveras. Tony, it picked up your confession." His heart rate quickened as many thoughts flashed through his mind. "Paul believed in the law, but he was fair. He was your partner. If he had evidence that you did something illegal, he would have given you an opportunity to turn yourself in. But instead, you took that opportunity to murder him before he could expose you."

Tony's eyes widened and his mouth went dry. Words escaped him for the next few moments. He finally stammered, "I…I just said that to…"

"Tony, say nothing," Carolyn said. "You are under arrest. You have the right to remain silent. Anything you say can and will be used against you in a court of law. You have the right to an attorney. If you cannot afford an attorney, one will…"

Roadblock on Memory Lane

I awoke with a headache almost too painful to bear,
as I used my hand to shield the sun's morning glare.

I massaged the back of my head knowing I took quite a lick
and spotted, just a few feet away, a sculptured walking stick.

Lying on my side, I struggled to make sense of it all.
Although I tried, there was simply nothing I could recall.

Because of barking and yelling, I could tell dogs and people
were near,
and within a moment, a man in a sheriff's badge did appear.

"Are you okay?" the sheriff asked, before I nodded yes.
"She's not so lucky," a deputy solemnly confessed.

I turned from my side and saw a woman's body for the first
time.
"The blue under the fingernails means poison," the deputy said,
indicating there was a crime.

I staggered to my feet, but quickly fell as if someone yelled,
"Timber!"
The sheriff said, "You need your walking stick to walk. Don't
you remember?"

I frantically crawled past a water bottle on the ground to see if
she was truly dead.
One look at the body and I knew she was deceased like the
deputy had said.

"Don't look. You've been through enough," the sheriff said,
ushering me away.
"And seeing someone you're so close to. It's too much all in
one day."

I scratched my head. "I've never seen this woman before in my
life."
The sheriff put his hand on my shoulder. "That was Julie, your
wife."

I must have fainted because I awoke in a crowded hospital room.
"Who are all you people!" I frantically yelled with a boom.

"I'm your best friend Mark," a forty year old man calmly said.
"And I'm Julie's sister, Sue," a thirty year old lady stated, sitting
on my bed.

"Oh," I said, not recognizing either Mark or Sue.
Mark declared, "We're going to find out who did this to you."

Sue explained, "We know you two left the campsite early to take
a walk.
Neither Mark or I followed because you said you two needed to
talk."

"Mark left to go fishing, but I stayed by the campsite," Sue stated.
"After you were gone for two hours, I knew that was too belated."

"When Mark later returned, we called the sheriff to search for you two.
The sheriff found Julie too late, but at least he found you."

"Wait a minute. Why would anyone want to kill Julie?" I asked Sue and Mark.
Sue took a deep breath and I knew on a long story she was about to embark.

"Julie was a wealthy scientist on the brink of the discovery of a revolutionary abortion pill
that would make abortion an easy and confidential way to kill."

"This made religious groups angry and she received a threatening death note.
But who was mad enough to kill her? Mark here is my vote."

"Damn you!" Mark said upset. "All because I'm the leader of the Right to Life fight.
But, you Sue, as Julie's sister and research assistant, sure had a motive alright."

"Okay, I admit it. I inherit all rights to the abortion pill.
But, that was it," Sue said. "That's all I got in the will."

The door was thrust open and the sheriff walked in as we all
looked confused.
The sheriff cleared his throat and announced, "I've identified the
poison that was used."

"Our murderer, it seems, believes in sick irony when they kill.
Because you see, the poison used was the lethal solution in
Julie's abortion pill."

"The solution was found in Julie's water bottle," the sheriff said.
"All it took was a few sips to leave Julie dead."

Sue's eyes widened and Mark's closed tight,
while my eyes wondered if there was a murderer in sight.

"That can't be!" Sue yelled. "That solution is impossible to
get."
"Impossible for most," the sheriff replied. "But easy for
someone close to Julie, you forget."

"What a painful way to go," Sue said with deep regret.
"It would have taken some time for the solution to take full
effect."

"She'd have chest pains, headaches and her mouth would have
gone dry,
and then she'd experience respiratory distress before three
minutes had gone by."

"I'm amazed with your knowledge of the solution," the sheriff
said with a frown.
"I think it's best that you come answer some questions
downtown."

As the sheriff and Sue left, Mark shot her a look of despise.
Mark asked me, "Do you suppose Sue is responsible for Julie's demise?"

"It's possible she poisoned Julie's water bottle," I slowly said.
"But, why, why would she have then hit me over the head?"

Mark said, "Julie always had the water bottle snapped to her belt which just doesn't fit.
That would mean to poison the bottle the murderer would have had to ask for it."

"My God!" I said. "That means Julie knew."
Mark turned serious. "You mean Julie realized it was Sue."

I shook my head. "Julie knew the symptoms of her drug."
"I don't get it. So what?" Mark said with a shoulder shrug.

Sweat poured down my face and I immediately felt weak.
Thoughts swirled around my mind, but I was unable to speak.

"Since Julie recognized the murderer and the symptoms, she would have reacted violently.
She would have grabbed anything she could," I thought to myself silently.

Experiencing those awful symptoms, any weapon she'd pick, even an ordinary sculptured walking stick.

Mark stared at me, wondering what I was thinking.
But, my thoughts disappeared as I felt my heart sinking.

My recollections of that fateful morning were still blank.
There was still an overdraft on my memory bank.

But now, I know a simple fact that would change my life.
Just this morning, I had intentionally killed my wife.

Love Hurts

I was sitting down at the desk in my private eye's office, just about to take the first sip of my Tuesday morning coffee. My lips touched the edge of the coffee mug and my nose inhaled the rich aroma of hot coffee. I closed my eyes as I took a slow sip, which was welcomed by my dry throat. I was thinking that this was the way every workday should start when Steve Granger burst through my office door. Startled, my right hand shook and I winced in pain as the hot coffee scalded the roof of my mouth.

"Robert, I need your help," Steve announced. Steve was a big, burly man with a mustache and beard. As I wiped my lips with a napkin, I glared at Steve, who was reaching into his pocket. He pulled out a folded note and placed it on my desk. "Read that. Josh wrote it."

Josh was the younger of Steve's two children. Twenty years ago, I introduced Steve to his future wife, Rachel, and have been close friends with both of them ever since. Their two sons had come to know me affectionately as Uncle Robert. I looked at the photocopied note, which read, "He shoved me down the stairs and threatened me. He said he could do worse. I hate him." Then, in all caps, "I HATE HIM."

I slowly lifted my head and looked at Steve, who stared right at me. "Well?" Steve said. "What do you think?"

My forehead wrinkled as I looked back down at the note. "It's a photocopy of a spiral note pad of some kind."

"It's from Josh's notepad. He uses it sort of like a diary. Writes random thoughts and experiences."

"Do you know when he wrote this?"

"Not exactly. There are no dates in the notepad, but this was the last written page so it has to be recent. He stayed at my house last night. When he was in the shower this morning, I noticed the notepad, sitting on the desk in his room."

A frown crossed my face as if I tasted something bitter. "And you read it?"

"I was curious. I'm not around in his everyday life any more. I wanted to know how things were going at home, you know, with Damon in the house." Damon was Rachel's new husband and Steve's favorite target of ridicule. Damon, according to Steve, was nothing more than a thirty something boy toy, who satisfied Rachel's mid-life crisis. It has been three months since Rachel remarried. Gesturing toward the note in my hand, Steve said, "I never thought I'd find anything like that. I didn't know what to do. I made a photocopy of the page and put the notepad back on his desk." As a self-employed real estate broker, Steve kept a small photocopier in his home office.

I studied the note before saying, "He wrote that he was shoved down the stairs. Did you see any bruises or marks on Josh?"

"No, but the note said he could do worse. I'm more worried about what may happen in the future."

I took a deep breath and exhaled audibly. "Did you ask Josh about the note?"

"I wanted to," Steve said, beginning to pace. "But, I know he would have been furious at me for reading his notepad. I just asked him if everything was okay at home and he said that it was." Steve looked directly at me, his eyes burning into mine. "Josh may be in real danger. I need you to find out who Josh fears in this note before something more serious happens." Steve pulled out his wallet. "You're a private eye. I'll pay your normal rate."

"Put your wallet away," I said, waving my right hand in the air. "You may be making a big deal out of nothing. But, if it will give you peace of mind, I'll check into it." I raised my eyebrows and dipped my head slightly. "Okay?"

Steve stood up, placed both hands on my desk and looked me right in the eye. "I really appreciate this."

I nodded my head and said, "I know…"

"No, you don't. I'm a fifty year old divorced father. My boys are my life." Steve paused a moment. "Do you know the worst thing about being separated from them?"

"No."

"Everyone thinks it's that I'm not around to have fun with them." Steve shook his head. "That's not it. It's that I'm not around to protect them, to make sure they're alright, you know." Steve's mouth quivered a bit as he added, "They can have fun with anyone: relatives, friends, classmates. But, to look after them and make sure they're okay…" Steve tapped his chest. "That's my job."

"I'll go over to the school this afternoon and get to the bottom of this," I said. I shook Steve's hand and walked him toward the door. Shoving the note in my pants pocket, I promised him that I would give him a call sometime tomorrow.

I was staked out in front of the high school parking lot when the bell rang at 3:00. Within a few minutes, students were flowing out of the school, excited that their school day had ended. I rested up against an old, black Jeep, which I recognized was Drew's, Steve's older son. I figured this was the best way to meet up with Josh, who usually got a ride home from his brother.

I spotted Drew among the sea of students exiting the school grounds. Drew, a star wide receiver on the varsity football team, stood out among the crowd. Thanks to many hours in the weight room and a recent growth spurt a year ago, Drew stood a muscular six feet tall. He was laughing with a friend about his size and build as he walked toward me. Drew, who wore blue jeans and a T-shirt, had a backpack draped over his right shoulder. Drew's face lit up when he saw me. "Uncle Robert, what are you doing here?"

Drew and I did our ritual high-five greeting before I responded, "I happened to be in the neighborhood."

Drew smiled before gesturing toward his friend. "Hey, this is my buddy and the guy who is going to throw me at least 15 touchdown passes this year, Percy Brown. Percy, my Uncle Robert, the best man I know."

"Nice to meet ya," Percy said, chewing gum. We shook hands. I had heard about this kid, Percy. The local papers had said that he was the best quarterback the school has had in the last decade. He wore a blue baseball cap, which was pressed down, in an upside down 'u' shape, over his forehead.

"Shouldn't you two be at football practice?" I asked.

"First week of school," Percy said with a smile. "Mercifully, Coach Fox gives us this week off."

I turned toward Drew. "Where's your brother?"

"He was supposed to meet me here right after school," Drew said, taking a look at his watch and then glancing back at the school. "He should be here any minute."

"Excuse us a minute," I said to Percy. I patted Drew on the back and led him away from Percy and the car. "How's everything at home, you know, with your mom's new husband?"

Drew shrugged before saying as he squinted, "It's okay, I guess."

"How's Josh handling it? I know how close he is to his father."

"Josh really misses him. When dad moved out about a year ago, it devastated him." Drew leaned closer to me. "Now, he only sees his father every other weekend."

"And Damon's not a good substitute?"

Drew snickered. "The drill sergeant? No way. He's my mom's husband, but he aint our father."

I nodded my head. "Have you ever seen Damon get physical with Josh?"

"Nah, never physical."

"What about at school? Has Josh gotten into any fights? Maybe trouble with a bully?"

"Nah," Drew said, shaking his head. "Josh isn't one to get into fights. And if a bully was bothering him, he would have come to me." Drew paused a moment to study my face. "Say, what's this all about?"

"Hey Drew!" Percy shouted from the car. "I want to get to the mall and check out those concert tickets. Let's go."

"I told you!" Drew shouted back at Percy. "We have to wait for Josh so we can drop him off at my house."

Percy sighed with displeasure. He folded his arms in front of his chest and leaned back on Drew's car.

I put my hand on Drew's shoulder. "I can stay and drop off Josh at your house if you like."

"You sure?"

"Yeah," I said with a nod. "It'll give me a chance to visit with him."

"Thanks!" Drew said, slapping me on the shoulder. "See you later." Drew walked back to the car and he and Percy drove off.

I decided to stay in the exact spot that Drew's car had been. As I waited, I saw most of the student parking lot empty out. I looked at my watch. It was now 3:15 and the trail of exiting students had vanished. Then, in the distance, I spotted Josh walking toward me. Josh, who had yet to hit his growth spurt like Drew, was about five foot five inches tall. He appeared a little tired, looking down at the ground as he slowly walked. He seemed to have the weight of the world (not just his heavy backpack) on his shoulders.

It wasn't until he was about fifty feet away that he noticed me. "Uncle Robert!" he said excitedly, before picking up his pace. When he reached me, we embraced. For a moment, he seemed happy and relaxed. He had curly, black hair and dimples on both cheeks when he smiled. Those dimples disappeared as he looked around, "Where's Drew? We were supposed to meet here after school."

"He left with his friend Percy," I said, which seemed to shift his disposition again.

"He left me?" Josh said in disbelief. "He did the same thing yesterday. I had to walk home."

"I told him to leave. I thought you and I could hang out. Hey! How'd you like to go to the ice cream parlor?"

"Cool!" Josh said as a smile and his characteristic dimples returned to his face.

As we drove to the ice cream parlor, I peppered Josh with questions about school and his home life. All his answers were short and to the point, usually answering with an "it's okay" or "it's fine". When we got to the ice cream parlor, I decided to stop my persistent inquiries. Instead, we began talking about the prospects of the local pro football team this year.

We were about half way through our ice cream sundaes when Josh asked me, "Is it wrong to keep a secret?"

My heart rate increased, but I kept my cool. I put my spoon down and looked right at Josh. "Well, that depends on the secret." I thought for a second before asking, "If you keep this secret, will anyone get hurt?" Josh shook his head. "And if you tell the secret, could someone get hurt?"

"Yeah."

"I see," I said, rubbing my face. "Is that someone you?" Josh looked down at his ice cream and slowly nodded. "So on one hand, you keep a secret and no one gets hurt. On the other hand, you tell and you could get hurt. So, why say anything?"

"Because it's the right thing to do," Josh said without hesitation.

I studied Josh's face and decided that I had to make my pitch. "Josh, if anyone has physically harmed you in any way, or even threatened to, you have to tell me." Josh just looked down, staring at what was left of his melted sundae. "Please Josh, tell me."

"I can't. I don't want to talk about it any more. I want to go home." Josh got up from his chair. Standing awkwardly, Josh waited for my next move.

"Okay," I said rising, before tossing a $10 bill on the table.

On the drive home, Josh was very quiet. Since he clearly was in no mood to talk, I dropped him off at his house, not bothering to come in. However, he showed a little life when I asked him, "How would you like me to come by tomorrow morning and give you a ride to school?"

"Cool," Josh said, flashing a smile before closing the passenger's side door.

The next morning, which was Wednesday, I pulled up to Josh's house a little after seven thirty. I had arrived early, on purpose, hoping to ask Rachel a few questions. When Rachel opened the door, she had a shocked expression on her face. "Robert. What a nice surprise!"

"Josh didn't tell you?" I said, still standing on the porch. "I promised I would take him to school today. May I come in?"

"Oh yes, of course," Rachel said, embarrassed. She led me to the living room as we sat down. Rachel, who was in her mid fifties, had always done a great job of fighting Father Time. A beautiful woman, she kept in great shape, which hid the fact that there was a 15-year difference between her and Damon. Smart and determined, Rachel was the strongest willed woman that I knew. Gesturing with her hand, she said, "Josh is upstairs getting dressed. Can I get you something to drink?"

"No, but I was hoping we could talk for a bit."

"Oh," Rachel said with raised eyebrows. She sat down, leaning forward with anticipation. "What's on your mind?"

"Josh seemed a little down when I saw him yesterday. How's everything working out, you know with Damon moving in and all?"

"We have good days and bad days, but, overall, it's okay."

"Bad days?"

"Well, just last week, Damon told him to turn the TV off and get to bed," Rachel said. "Josh stormed upstairs, yelling that he wanted to live with his dad."

"Josh is at the age where he wants and needs a strong male role model. I think it's natural that he'd want to be with his dad." I paused a moment. "I'm glad he has Drew. How are they getting along?"

"Great, Drew really loves his younger brother. There isn't anything he wouldn't do for him," Rachel said. "And Josh, he wants to spend as much time as possible with Drew, especially now that they are going to the same school."

"That sounds great. Did Josh try out for the freshman football team?"

"He did, but Coach Fox cut him during the last day of summer tryouts. Josh was disappointed, but I think Drew took it even harder than he did."

My heart dropped, as I thought about all of the things Josh has had to deal with. "I'd like to spend a little more time with him. Do you mind if I pick Josh up after school today?"

"That would be great. I'll tell Drew that he's off the hook."

"Hey there!" a voice boomed walking down the stairs. It was Damon, decked out in a full Marine officer's uniform. Damon looked like a military man, clean-shaven face, short, crew cut black hair, and a buff body. "I thought I heard your voice."

"Look who's all dressed up," I said, as I shook his hand. He had the firmest handshake of any man I had ever met.

"I'm speaking at two local high schools today about the benefits of joining the Marines. I have to dress for the occasion."

"I'll check what's keeping Josh," Rachel said as she headed upstairs.

"I see you've done some redecorating," I said, gesturing toward the mantle case with an automatic rifle in a large glass case. "I'm guessing this is yours."

"Yeah," Damon said, walking over to the case. He lightly tapped the case as he said, "This is the gun I had when I served active duty. This baby saved my life. It means a lot to me."

"Keeping it in the living room? Is that safe?"

"The case is locked. Besides, I don't keep bullets in the gun. So, nothing to worry about." He glanced at his watch. "I better see what's holding Josh up. It was really nice seeing you."

We shook hands again, before he headed upstairs. I walked over to inspect the bottom steps, walls, and banister. There were marks, but I couldn't tell if it was from normal wear and tear or whether someone had fallen down them recently.

"Uncle Robert," Josh said, jogging down the stairs with a smile on his face.

"Don't forget your lunch!" Rachel yelled from upstairs. Josh jogged into the kitchen, grabbed a paper bag, and led me out the door. In the car ride to school, Josh was very talkative and you would never know that he was agonizing about telling a secret just sixteen hours before.

When we arrived at the school, Josh reached for the door, but I quickly said, "Hold on a minute!" He turned and looked at me.

"I talked it over with your mom. You and I are going to hit the batting cages after school."

"Cool."

"I'll pick you up right at 3:00, so don't be late."

"I won't," Josh said.

"And one more thing," I said, pointing at Josh. "I'll pick you up over by the gym at the south side of campus, not in the school parking lot. There's a lot less cars over there." Josh nodded before hopping out of the car. Josh looked back to wave before turning to walk toward school. Once Josh had disappeared in the distance, I drove back to my office and called Steve to inform him of my investigations and the fact I was meeting with Josh again this afternoon after school.

"Well, I really appreciate you looking into this," Steve said to me over the phone. "You know, you barely caught me. I have to drive to Shreveport to look at a bunch of properties and I'll be on the road all day. I can call you when I get back home around five o'clock."

"Sounds great," I said before hanging up.

I looked at my watch as I patiently waited in my car at the south side of the high school. It was 3:20. I turned off the radio and jumped out of the car. I put my hand up to shield my eyes from the sun. There was no sign of Josh. Had he forgotten I was going to pick him up? I rubbed my face as I momentarily became concerned. He was really late, even for Josh. I decided to go looking for him. I slowly walked onto the campus, pausing a moment any time I thought a lone student might be Josh. I wandered aimlessly before finally deciding to head to the administration building at the far north side of campus.

It was after three thirty when I entered the main office. A middle-aged woman with glasses near the edge of her nose stood behind the front counter. "May I help you?"

"I was supposed to pick up a Josh Granger right after school, but he didn't show up where we were supposed to meet."

"Josh Granger?" the woman said with wrinkled forehead. "Are you his father?"

"No. I'm Robert Douglas, a very close friend of the family."

"I see," the woman said slowly. "I'm Melissa, the school nurse. Josh has been roughed up a bit." I let out a small gasp as I put my hand over my heart. "He's okay," Melissa quickly added. "I'll take you to him." My heart rate quickened as I followed the woman down a hallway to a small room where Josh was resting. He laid, near motionless, with a large ice pack applied to his upper face. I noticed a busted lip and bruises around his jaw and right side of his lower face.

Not to disturb him, I whispered to Melissa from the corner of the room, "How did this happen?"

"We don't know. According to his sixth period teacher, he was fine. That class ended at 2:45. Sometime between then and about 3:00, someone beat him up pretty badly." I looked back at Josh and shook my head in disbelief, frustration, and anger. The nurse continued, "Coach Fox saw him lying by the gym area, in this state and brought him here."

"Did Josh say what happened to him?"

"No," the nurse said, shaking her head. "I took some x-rays of his face. There are no broken bones. And we have already called both his parents. Mrs. Granger is on her way now."

"Someone assaulted him. Have the police been called?" I asked. The nurse had a blank expression on her face. "I'll call them. I have a friend at the station." I started back toward the hallway.

"Hold on, you'll need this," Melissa said as she walked over to a desk drawer. "I took a picture documenting the injuries." I swallowed hard as I looked at the picture. A large portion of his face was bruised. He sported a black right eye. His right side of his face was so swollen, it appeared that Josh had trouble fully opening his right eye.

"Thank you," I said as I put the picture in my coat pocket.

"Oh my gosh," a voice said behind me. It was Rachel, who covered her mouth with her hand. She slowly walked into the room and knelt beside Josh. She lifted the ice bag from his face and shrieked, which woke Josh up. She asked him, "What happened?"

"Mom," Josh mumbled as he squinted with his right eye. "I don't want to talk about it."

Rachel turned and looked at me and asked the same question. "The only thing that we know is that someone beat him up pretty badly near the gym area after his last class."

Rachel looked back at her son. "Josh honey, you have to tell us. Who did this to you?" Josh turned his head slightly to look at his mother. "Please. Tell us."

"I really don't want to talk about it," Josh said, turning his head slightly away.

Rachel was clearly frustrated. I motioned for her to come over toward me. I led her back to the hallway.

"Why won't he tell us what happened?" she asked.

"I don't know, but don't put too much pressure on him. I'll get to the bottom of this, I promise. You should take him home and I'll go by the police department. I have a friend who is a deputy. I'll have him do some investigations."

"Sounds good," Rachel said before hugging me.

It was almost four o'clock when I arrived at the police station, where I heard someone shout, "Come on, this is so bogus!" and another voice shout back, "You better calm down, son!"

When I opened the door, I immediately recognized the two men who were shouting. "Hey!" I yelled, stepping in between

Drew and a senior deputy named Michael Petersen. I looked at Officer Petersen. "I know this boy. Let me handle this."

Officer Petersen moved closer to me and said, "Sheriff Drake is out sick today, so I'm in charge. I don't have time to put up with any crap. If you don't settle him down, I'm going to throw him out of here."

I nodded to Petersen before slowly walking over to Drew. I put both of my hands on his shoulders. "Calm down and tell me what's going on."

"You know Percy over there," Drew said, gesturing to his friend, who was sitting down at a desk with another officer. Percy smiled uneasily as he waved awkwardly with handcuffed hands. "They're making a capital offense out of a case of mistaken identity. He didn't do it."

"Do what?" I asked.

"They say he broke into the school snack shack after school on Monday, but that can't be true. We have last period together. We went from our last class and we drove to the mall. He was with me the whole time." Drew put his right hand up and added, "I swear."

"This is nothing to get worked up about," I said softly. "I doubt the police will do anything serious."

"But, they won't release him until one of his parents picks him up."

"Sounds reasonable."

"You don't understand. Percy's dad is a tyrant with a terrible temper. He's warned Percy that if he gets into any more trouble, he'll yank him off the football team. This is his senior year."

I pulled Drew further toward the corner and whispered, "Alright, I'll stay and try to get Percy out of this mess, but right now, I need you to do something."

"Anything," Drew said immediately.

Once again, I put hands on his shoulder and looked him straight in the eye. "Promise me you won't freak out."

Drew rolled his eyes. "I promise."

"Okay," I said with a nod. "Earlier today, someone beat up Josh pretty badly…"

"What?!" Drew said, his eyes widening in disbelief. I glared at Drew as if to remind him of his promise. Drew took a deep breath to calm down. His eyes locked in on mine as he asked, "Who did it?"

"That's what I need your help with," I said as calmly as I could. "Josh won't talk to me or his mother about the incident. But, I know he'll talk to you. He should be home now. I need you to go home and get him to tell you what happened." Drew nodded his head. "I'll be there as soon as I get Percy out of this mess."

"Alright. I really appreciate you helping Percy out." Drew walked toward Percy. "Hey, Percy! I gotta go, but my uncle is going to stay and make sure things get worked out here. Okay?"

"Thanks man," Percy said, raising his chin slightly.

I realized that I had taken on two cases: one for Steve and now one for Drew.

After Drew left, I met with Officer Petersen alone in his small office. As we walked past Percy, Petersen said to another deputy to "finish fingerprinting the suspect and then lock him up." After we sat down, we both looked at each other, waiting for the other to speak. In his late twenties, the handsome deputy with short black hair was a fitness fanatic and had become quite the heartthrob among young ladies in the town. In my profession, it is critical to develop a solid working relationship with the local police department. Over the years, we have helped each other in a large number of cases.

Frustrated by the silent, staring game, Petersen finally spoke. "I know you're trying to help your nephew, but this boy, Percy, he's a punk. The school has a list of stuff he's done. Cut classes, cheated on an exam, talked back to a teacher…"

"But, he didn't break into the snack shack," I said, wagging my finger. "Because he was with my nephew, and my nephew wouldn't lie."

Petersen reached for a file on his desk. Looking at a file, he said, "School says they had a witness. Didn't give a name though."

"Their witness was mistaken. Drew swears he was with him. Come on, this is petty theft at best. You're handcuffing him, fingerprinting him." I tilted my head and squinted at Petersen. "What gives?"

"Alright," he said, sitting up in his chair. "I'll tell you. The school asked us to scare him a bit. They aren't pressing charges, but given this kid's track record, they thought maybe feeling handcuffs and the inside of a jail for a few minutes would do him some good."

"Now that you had some fun at the kid's expense," I said unimpressed with what Petersen was doing. "Why don't you release him to me?"

Petersen shook his head. "I'm only releasing him to his parents."

"Come on. Haven't you done enough to this kid?"

"We've barely done anything," Petersen said defensively. "We picked him up at the principal's office after school today. He hasn't been here more than twenty minutes."

"Okay, but as a personal favor to me," I said, putting my right hand over my heart. "Don't call his parents and release him to me. Please."

"It's too late. I called his father fifteen minutes ago. He'll be here any minute."

"Percy!" a voice roared from outside the office. Petersen and I headed out of his office. At the front of the station stood a bulky, red-faced man who appeared to be steaming with anger. The man, who had a shaved bald head, had both fists clenched tightly.

"May I help you, sir," Petersen said.

"I'm Stanley Brown, Percy's father." Wearing blue jeans and a striped shirt, he appeared to work in construction. "You have my son in custody."

"Yes, I'm deputy Petersen. We talked on the phone." After reviewing the man's identification, Petersen called to another officer to get Percy.

As soon as Percy came into view, Mr. Brown said angrily, "The police told me what you did. I swear I have had it with you."

"Dad, I swear, I didn't do it."

"Shut up." Mr. Brown flashed an intimidating glare, making the slightly taller Percy cower. The man turned to Petersen. "Tell me what I have to do to get him out of here."

"Since the school is not pressing charges, you can just take him," Petersen said.

After Petersen uncuffed Percy, Mr. Brown grabbed his son and yanked him toward the exit, muttering, "You're going to get it."

"Excuse me," I said as I stepped in between them and the door. "My nephew was with your son when the police say he broke into the snack shack. So, you should know this is all a misunderstand…"

"Yeah, right!" Mr. Brown said before walking past me with Percy along side of him.

I was disappointed that I failed in my mission to save Percy from his father. But, I reminded myself what I was really here to do: keep my promise to Steve about watching over his boys. Josh had already been hurt and I had to get to the bottom of this and fast. When I delivered the bad news about Josh to Steve tonight, I wanted to be able to tell him who was responsible.

Petersen walked over to me. "Sorry I couldn't help you more."

"Well," I said with a sigh. "I actually came down for another reason. Josh Granger, who is like my nephew, was brutally assaulted today at his school."

"I'm sorry to hear that. But, a school fight…"

"It wasn't a fight." I showed Petersen a picture of Josh's badly beaten face. Petersen, who has seen many horrific pictures in his time, still paused a moment, clearly affected by the picture. "It was an assault and it was premeditated," I said before handing him Josh's note.

Petersen slowly read it before looking back up at me. "From this, it would appear Josh knew who threatened him. Who did he say it was?"

"I can't get him to talk, but I'm gonna keep working on him. In the meantime, let's call Coach Fox. He found Josh lying on the ground. He might be able to give us a clue."

"Worth a try," Petersen said as he looked up the coach's number. "Here we go." He put the phone on speaker, dialed the number, and after three rings, Coach Fox's answering machine came on. Petersen left a message requesting the coach to call him back at the police station and saying that "it was regarding Josh Granger."

After Petersen hung up, I got up. "Thanks. I'm going back to Rachel Granger's house. If you learn anything new, please call me there." Petersen nodded before I headed out of his office.

When I arrived at Rachel's home, I saw Drew getting in his jeep, which was parked in the driveway. He was starting up his jeep and I quickly parked my car on the street, blocking his exit. I jumped out of the car and raced over to the jeep.

"Hey! Where are you going? I told you to stay here and get Josh to tell you who hit him."

Drew looked directly at me as he said, "He told me."

"He did? Who hit him?"

Drew stared at me for a few seconds. "I can't tell you. This is something I need to take care of myself."

"What? No way. Whoever beat Josh up like that could do the same to you." I took a step closer, putting both hands on the rolled down window. "You need to tell me who hit Josh right now. I can get the police to pick this person up."

"I don't trust the police," Drew said. "Say, did they release Percy to you?"

I dropped my head. "No, his father picked him up and took him home."

"See how useful the police are! Sometimes, if you want things done right, you have to do it yourself." Drew peeled out of the driveway running over the front lawn, off the curb, past my car, and onto the street.

I was frozen in shock with Drew's brazen maneuver. I gathered myself and raced to my car. However, by the time I started my car and turned around, I had lost Drew. I had no choice but to go back to Rachel's house.

After Rachel let me into the house, I asked her, "Do you know where Drew went?"

"No. He raced out about five minutes ago. I was upstairs with Josh. Drew was downstairs and he yelled that he had somewhere to go."

I covered my face with both hands. "So, he didn't tell you?"

"Tell me what?"

"Who beat Josh up."

"No," Rachel said, before a realization hit her. "My God, Drew knows! He was alone with Josh for a few moments when I refilled his ice bag. That's when Josh must have told him."

I turned around to pace nervously as I clasped both hands together over my head. "Drew was pretty upset. He may be in danger. You know how he…" I stopped mid sentence.

"What?"

I pointed to the rifle case. It was empty. "Did Drew take that?"

"I don't know."

"This has gone far enough," I muttered before heading upstairs. Rachel followed me as I entered Josh's room. I sat on the edge of his bed and looked at him. "Okay, the time for secrets is over. You told Drew who beat you up." I leaned closer to Josh with an intimidating glare. "Now, tell me."

"I can't," Josh said, refusing to even look at me.

Frustrated, I looked over at Rachel. She nodded to me as if to say it was okay for me to push further. "Josh! We know that someone threatened you and shoved you down the stairs." Josh turned toward me, appearing surprised. "We also know that the same person that shoved you, wanted you to keep a secret and then, he beat you up today. Now, you told your brother and he hightailed it out of here to confront this person. If you care at all about your brother's safety, you'll tell us what you told him."

"Drew told me not to say anything to anyone, okay. He said he would take care of it." The trust and faith Josh had in Drew was incredible. Nothing Rachel or I could say was going to convince Josh to talk to us. Finally, we gave up and left Josh alone. I knew the only person who could get Josh to talk now was his father.

It was four forty-five, fifteen minutes before Steve had said he would be back from his business trip. Thinking he might have come home early, I called him on his home phone. But, on the fourth ring, his answering machine picked it up. After the tone, I said, "Hey Steve, this is Robert. It's very important that I talk to you. As soon as you get in, call me at Rachel's house. It's about your boys." I hung up the phone and then scratched my head, wondering if I could have left a better message. I had purposely left out details because I knew he would go ballistic.

Rachel lightly patted me on the back and suggested we go to Drew's room to see if we could gather any clues to where he went. Rachel grabbed the school's yearbook and we looked through it to see if anyone triggered in Rachel's mind who would want to do harm to Josh.

"There's one thing I don't understand," I said. "If it were a bully at school, why wouldn't Josh come right out and tell us. I mean, why all of the secrecy?"

Before Rachel could answer, we heard a door slam downstairs. We immediately jumped up and saw Drew coming up the stairs. My eyes bulged out and my heart dropped at the sight before me. Drew sported a black eye and a bruise on the right side of his face. His face was not as bad off as Josh's, but it was bad. Drew's right hand clutched his stomach as he bent over slightly as he walked. "What happened to you?" Rachel asked.

"Don't want to talk about it," Drew said, going into Josh's room and slamming the door behind him. Rachel tried to open the door, but he had already locked it.

"Drew!" Rachel exclaimed, knocking hard on the door. "Open this door." There was no response. Frustrated and with no other option, we camped outside Josh's door for the next five minutes until the door finally opened.

With Josh holding a suitcase in his hand, Drew led Josh out the door. Josh held an ice pack up to his face. "Where do you think you're going?" Rachel asked with her hands on her hips.

"It's not safe here," Drew said, walking past us and heading to the stairs.

I looked at Rachel, who motioned for me to catch up with Drew. I raced down the stairs, grabbing a hold of Drew before he could reach the door. "This has gone on long enough," I said, looking at Drew's bruised face. "Who hit you? Tell me right now."

Drew sighed before looking at Josh. He looked back at me and said, "It was Damon."

"Damon?!" Rachel exclaimed in shock.

"Yes," Drew said, looking directly at his mom. "He beat Josh up after school earlier today."

Rachel turned to her youngest son. "Is this true?" Josh nodded his head. Rachel held her hand in front of her dropped jaw.

"What happened to you?" I asked Drew.

"I went over to Damon's office to confront him and ask him why he beat up Josh. I saw him in the parking lot and I told him to keep his hands off my brother. When I shoved him, he went nuts, completely out of control. He began hitting me over and over. After he was done, he said he'd kill me if I told anyone."

"Alright, you two are coming with me to the police station." Drew was about to speak, but I immediately said, "No arguments." I turned to Rachel. "You should come as well."

"No. I want to be here to confront Damon when he returns."

I grimaced. "I don't think that is such a good id…"

"I'll be fine. Go."

"Promise me you'll call the station as soon as he arrives," I said, looking directly at her.

"I promise." She motioned with her hand. "Now, go."

Drew, Josh and I loaded into my car and I drove to the police department. Josh and Drew explained their stories to Petersen while I was giving my statements in a separate room. After I was done, I asked the deputy to take me to Drew and Josh. He led me to the adjacent room. Petersen, still questioning the boys, waved me in.

After I sat down, Drew said, "Josh and I, we can never go back to that house with Damon living there. It's not safe there."

Drew looked at Josh. "My brother and I want to live with our father. Can you make that happen?"

Petersen leaned forward. "That'll be for a court to decide. But, until then, I'll make sure you two are safe. When we're done here, Robert will take you to your father's house."

"Sure thing," I said, which made Josh smile.

At that moment, another police officer, accompanied by a silver-haired man with a smile, entered. "Sorry to interrupt, but this is John Fox. You had called him earlier."

A physically fit Coach John Fox entered, intent on greeting Petersen. However, he stopped short when he recognized Drew and Josh. Seeing Drew's bruised face, he immediately asked him as knelt down, "My gosh, what happened to you?"

"Kind of a long story," Drew said, avoiding going into details.

"Are you okay?"

"I'm fine, coach," Drew said. After Coach Fox flashed him a skeptical look, Drew added, wide-eyed, "Really."

As Coach Fox slowly stood up, Petersen asked his fellow officer to escort the boys out to sign some paperwork. I stayed in the room with Petersen to hear what the coach had to say.

"Have a seat," Petersen said, gesturing toward one of the guest chairs. Coach Fox sat down, crossing his leg. "I contacted you because, at the time, Josh refused to tell us who inflicted his injuries."

"He stonewalled me too," Coach Fox said. "I really have no idea. I must have asked him five times on the way to the nurse's office."

"I see," Petersen said, pausing. "Well, he finally told us so I..."

"He did? Who beat him up?"

Petersen fiddled with a pencil in his right hand. "We're in the midst of an investigation. It would be inappropriate for me to say." Petersen put the pencil down and slowly rose from his chair. "Well, I'm sorry you came all the way down here for no reason."

"Hold on," a still seated Coach Fox said. "There was another reason that I came down here." Petersen raised his eyebrows before slowly sitting back down. "Stanley Brown called me about 45 minutes ago. He said that he was pulling his son Percy off the team. He said he got into some trouble with the police?"

"Yeah, and?" Petersen said slowly.

"Well," Coach Fox said, realizing Petersen was going to make him work for any information. "He just said that he was pulling Percy off the football team this year to teach him a lesson." He scratched the back of his neck before saying, "I was hoping you could tell me what lesson Percy needed."

Petersen looked at me and I gestured with my head to tell the coach. "He was suspected of breaking into the school snack shack," Petersen finally said.

"Suspected? Was he charged with anything?"

"No, he wasn't," Petersen replied.

"Wait a minute. What makes you suspect him in the first place?"

"Someone witnessed it," Petersen said.

"Who?" the coach asked immediately.

"Can't say," Petersen said, not admitting that he didn't actually know.

Coach Fox sighed and shook his head. "I don't know if you realize what you've done. By telling his father this, you're ruining this boy's life. If he doesn't play his senior year, there goes any college scholarship. The kid has a chance to be a real star in college, maybe even in the pros. You're letting that be thrown away because of some misunderstanding."

"What do you want me to do?" Petersen asked, folding his arms.

"If you're not arresting him, you must have some doubts," Coach Fox said. "Call Percy's father. Tell him you don't think Percy did it and he shouldn't be punished."

"He has a point," I said from the corner. "We are talking about this kid's life."

"Okay," Petersen said, relenting. "I'll talk to Mr. Brown."

Just as Petersen was escorting Coach Fox out, another officer came in and said to me, "Call for you. It's Rachel. Line 2."

"Thanks," I said before picking up a nearby phone. Now, alone in the room, I closed the door to Petersen's office. "Hi, Rachel," I said as I pressed the receiver up against my ear.

"Hi Robert," Rachel said in a lowered voice. "Two things. First, Steve returned your call from earlier. He was at home. I didn't tell him what's going on because I was afraid how he'd react."

"Good thinking. I'll deal with Steve. And what was the second thing?"

"Damon's home," Rachel replied. A shot of adrenaline coursed through my body. "Robert, I've never seen him like this before. He's so upset."

"Why? You didn't tell him that we know he beat up the boys."

"No, it's not that. He noticed his rifle was missing. He started yelling about which of the two boys took it. I mean, he was really mad. Right now, he's in the bedroom changing."

"Rachel, I want you out of that house. I'll get Petersen to send a squad car down right now."

"Good," Rachel replied. "But, I have to stay to ensure he doesn't leave."

"I really think you should leave…"

"Oh, he's coming downstairs. Get a car down here," Rachel said before hanging up.

For a moment, I stood there dumbfounded, listening to the dial tone. Petersen re-entered the room and noticed my expression. Before he could speak, I blurted out, "That was Rachel. Damon is back at the house."

"No problem. I'll go pick him up right now."

"Thanks," I said, relieved Petersen was going to take care of it personally. I started toward the door, but Petersen stopped me.

"There's just one thing that's bothering me," he said. "In addition to the bruises on his face, Drew had abrasions on his right hand."

"He probably got them when Damon was beating him up," I offered.

"Yeah, that's what Drew said." There was an awkward pause as we just looked at each other for a few seconds. "It's just the abrasions were only on his right hand, which seems to suggest they came from offensive rather than defensive actions."

"If Drew said he got them in his altercation with Damon, then that's what happened."

"Okay," Petersen said slowly. "But who was doing most of the hitting, Damon or Drew?" I thought about his statement as he looked at his watch. "I better pick Damon up," Petersen said. "I'm done with the boys. You should take them to their father's house now."

I rang the doorbell at Steve's house and nervously waited. I took a deep breath and went over in my mind the words that I wanted to say. I knew he would be angry at the sight of his beaten sons.

"Robert!" Steve said with a smile, as he opened the door. He noticed his sons and his entire expression changed. "What happened? Are you guys okay?"

"We're fine," Drew responded.

Steve turned his attention toward Josh. "Let me see," Steve said, taking off the ice pack, which covered the right side of his face. Steve gasped at the sight. "Who did this to you?"

Josh looked at Drew, who answered, "It was Damon."

"I'll kill him!" Steve started back in the house and toward the garage, but I caught up to him.

"The police are arresting him right now," I said just before Steve hit the button to open the garage. He continued toward his car, seemingly ignoring me. To be heard over the noise of the garage door opening, I shouted, "I thought you wanted to protect your boys! They are here, and you're running out on them!"

Steve stopped to glare at me. "Don't question how I care for my boys! I came to you to watch over Josh and look what happened!"

"No, you asked me to figure out who threatened Josh. Now, we know it was Damon, who unfortunately followed through on that threat. But, he is being arrested right now." I pointed back toward the house and said, "You are needed here to make sure your sons are okay, physically and emotionally."

Steve banged the hood of his car. "I hate it when you're right," he muttered as he passed me on his way back into the house.

Steve called a friend who was a doctor. Within ten minutes, he arrived and looked them both over. He said that they both would be okay, but should probably rest at home for a few days.

I walked the doctor to the door. Just as I was about to close the door, I saw Petersen's patrol car parking on the street in front of the house. With Steve occupied with his boys, I closed the door and met Petersen outside on the porch.

"I figured you'd be here," Petersen said. "I have some news."

"What is it?"

"One of the deputies found Damon's gun. It was on the side of the house. No bullets were in the gun."

"How did it get there?"

"Don't know," Petersen said with a shrug. "But, I wanted to let you know that we did not arrest Damon."

"You didn't? Why not?"

"For starters, no physical evidence. There wasn't a mark on him. Not even a scratch. Now, I can see how Damon may be able to beat up Josh without any marks, but not Drew."

"That's far from conclusive. Did you know that Damon was on the high school campus that afternoon, talking to students about the military? That puts him at the scene of the crime."

"Yeah, I know, but look at these photographs." Petersen showed me two photographs, one each of the Drew and Josh's beaten faces. "Look at their bruises. They're almost all on the right side of their face. That means that the attacker is most likely left handed. Damon is right handed. That means your two boys are lying."

"Why would they lie?" I asked, handing him back the photographs.

"Well, by framing Damon, they likely would be able to live with their dad and at the same time, they protect the person who really did it." As Petersen talked, I looked back through the porch window to see Steve hug Josh.

"That doesn't make sense," I said, still looking at the embrace. "Why would the boys lie to protect someone who beat them up?"

Petersen noticed my attention was diverted. He looked in the window as well. "They would if it were their father."

"So, Steve beat them up?" I asked, looking at him as if he were crazy.

"Yes. He forces them to say it was Damon. Then, he's sure to take custody away from Rachel and her abusive husband."

"That makes no sense. If Steve did this, Josh and Drew would want nothing to do with him."

"Are you sure about that?" Petersen asked. "There's one more thing. Steve is left handed."

"Well, it's a nice theory, but I've been looking at Steve over the last hour. He couldn't have done it. He doesn't have a scratch on him," I said, folding my arms in front of my chest.

"Three words: Alpha Male syndrome."

"What are you talking about?" I asked, briefly closing my eyes to temper my frustration.

"Alpha male syndrome," Petersen repeated. "In the animal kingdom, when a fight starts with an alpha male, the subordinate male won't fight back. He'll just take the punishment. Steve is clearly an alpha male over his boys. They wouldn't have fought back against their father."

"Sounds more like psycho-babble rather than real life."

"How's this for real life? Stanley Brown," Petersen said. "I took Coach Fox's advice and stopped by the Brown residence. You know, to tell Mr. Brown that I thought Percy was likely innocent and he shouldn't be punished."

"Yeah," I said slowly.

"Mr. Brown beat his son up really badly. Small man like that, did a real number on his bigger son. Percy didn't fight back."

"I warned you that guy was a loose cannon. Did you arrest Mr. Brown for beating his son?"

"He wasn't home," Petersen responded, sighing meekly. "But that's not my point. My point is that Percy is adamant about protecting his dad. That's the thing about abused sons. They stand behind their abusive fathers to the end."

"What did Percy say?"

"He gave me some story about 'running into a door'. Without Percy's testimony, it's going to be hard to make a case."

"Hard to make what case?" Steve asked, walking onto the porch and startling us. Steve looked at Petersen. "You did arrest Damon, right?"

"Mr. Granger, I'm very sorry about your boys," Petersen said, dipping his head slightly. "I'm committed to finding the culprit, but I'm not sure Damon is guy we're after."

"What are you talking about? Of course he is. Didn't Drew and Josh tell you he beat them up?"

"Yes, they did," Petersen said. "There are just a few things I need to straighten out before I can make an arrest. But, I promise you I will get to the bottom of this." Steve looked at Petersen with squinting eyes, seemingly unconvinced. "I will be in touch with you, sir," Petersen said to Steve, touching the bill of his cap. He turned to walk back to his car.

As we watched Petersen drive away, I said to Steve, "The boys said Damon beat them up, but did they say why he did it?"

"As a matter of fact, they did," Steve said. "Damon went off on Josh because Josh took his precious gun out of the case."

"That's the reason Josh gave you."

"Yeah," Steve replied. "He just told me a few minutes ago."

"When did he say that he took the gun?"

"Just this morning before school, he took it out and left..."

"He's lying. I was over there this morning and I drove him to school. That gun was locked in the case when I left, with Josh."

Steve looked at me cross-eyed as if he were trying to put the pieces to a complex puzzle together. "Why would Josh lie about stealing the gun?"

"To create a motive for Damon. Implicating Damon likely means he'll get to live with you."

Steve paused to think. "This is unbelievable. If Damon didn't beat Josh up, then who did?"

I held my index finger in the air. "Give me a few minutes with the boys and hopefully I'll be able to answer that question."

Steve nodded. "If your boys are lying, they're going to be in a lot of trouble unless we catch them right now, so they can recant their statements. This thing could go to trial and you don't want a defense attorney proving they committed perjury on the stand. They could get jail time."

"I understand," Steve said, taking a deep breath before exhaling audibly.

Steve and I walked into the living room. I turned the TV off and stood in front of them with my hands on my hips.

"Hey, what gives?" Drew said. "We were watching that."

"Just listen to what he has to say," Steve said, which immediately pacified Drew.

I walked over to Josh in the reclined lounge chair and knelt next to him. "Why did Damon attack you at school?"

"It was because I took his gun out of the case this morning," Josh said. "I knew that he hid the key to the case in the desk drawer."

"Why did you take his gun?" I asked.

"I don't know. I just wanted to see what it felt like to hold. I took it outside. Then, my mom called me for breakfast. I left it outside and never had a chance to put it back before school."

There was silence in the room as I stared at Josh. "Yeah," Drew said awkwardly. "When I confronted Damon, he said Josh needed to be taught a lesson in respecting others' property."

"You both are lying," I said, glaring at Josh and Drew. "I know because I saw the gun in the case when I took you to school today." I leaned in a little closer to Josh. "The lies have to stop. You can get in a lot of trouble here."

Josh looked over at his father and then to his brother. "My head hurts. I need to lie down," Josh said, before running toward the bedroom. I headed after him, but was intercepted by Drew.

"You should leave him alone," Drew said. "I think he's been through enough today."

"Whatever he has been through has been brought out partially by his lies, and yours," I said to Drew. Not wanting a physical confrontation with Drew, I walked back over to the sofa. Drew followed, sitting back down on a nearby sofa. "I know that you and Josh concocted this story about the gun and Damon. When you lie in one instance, people are going to distrust you in other areas." I paused and contemplated another angle. "Now, the police think your father was the one that beat you two up."

"What?" Drew said with wrinkled forehead. "That's ridiculous. My dad never laid a hand on me or my brother."

"On that point, I believe you, but I need you to be 100% honest with me. Who hit you?"

"Tell him the truth," Steve said.

Drew looked me in the eye for a while before shaking his head. "I already told you what happened. It was Damon. He beat my brother up and he beat me up."

Steve and I looked at each other. I shrugged my shoulders, not knowing where to go from here. Steve spoke up, thanking Drew for his honesty and asked him to check on his brother. Once Drew left, Steve suggested that I let "his boys get some rest" before walking me to the door. "You still don't believe them?"

"No," I said. "Damon didn't do it."

"As much as I'd like the boys to live with me, I don't want to take them away from Rachel on false pretenses."

"Call Rachel. Let her know what we think is going on."

"I will," Steve said. "In the meantime, I want you to figure out who really beat them up. You need to do it before Damon is wrongly accused and the boys commit perjury."

The next morning I was sitting in a local coffee shop eating breakfast with Officer Petersen. He broke the news to me that his discussions with Stanley Brown last night went nowhere. Petersen's plan to instill doubt in Mr. Brown's mind about whether Percy broke into the snack shack had failed. That was a major setback for me. If I got Percy back on the football team, I thought Drew might confide in me about what really happened to Josh.

I looked at the photographs of Drew and Josh's bruised faces. "This is so weird. All in one afternoon, Josh, Drew and Percy all get beaten up." I shook my head as I continued to study the photographs. "Like we said before, most of Drew and Josh's bruises are on the right side of their faces. You saw Percy. Where were his bruises?"

"Predominantly on the left side of his face," Petersen said. "So, his attacker was likely right handed. And surprise, surprise. His father, Mr. Brown, is right handed."

"Did Mr. Brown seem upset when you confronted him about Percy's bruises?" Petersen shook his head. "See, that's weird. I mean, when Steve learned his sons were hurt, he screamed for justice. That's what a father does, if he's innocent."

"Unless Mr. Brown believed that Percy deserved those bruises. Maybe he did."

"What?"

"There's something you need to know. This morning I called the school to find out who witnessed Percy breaking into the snack shack."

"Yeah," I said, before drinking some coffee. "Who was our mystery witness?"

"Josh Granger," Petersen said with raised eyebrows.

I put my coffee mug down and fell back in my chair. "Josh?"

"Yep, Josh. He says he saw Percy break into the school's snack shack and Drew says Percy was with him off campus."

Petersen leaned closer to me. "So, you tell me. Which one of your nephews is telling the truth?"

I buried my face in my hands. I felt like screaming in utter frustration. "I used to trust Drew, but every time I turn around, I catch him in a lie. And Josh, he hasn't really leveled with me on anything over the last few days."

"Let's suppose for a minute that Josh is lying," Petersen said. "Maybe Drew beat up Josh for framing his friend."

I shook my head and showed Petersen Josh's photograph. "Drew would never beat up his brother like this."

"You sure?" Petersen said, tilting his head. "Remember, Drew had abrasions on his right hand. That could have happened when he was beating Josh up." I began to shake my head again when Petersen, said, "Just hear me out. If Percy gets thrown off the football team, where does that leave Drew? I mean, it's Drew's senior year. How good can a star receiver be if he has to play with a backup QB."

"Okay," I said. "Then, tell me this. Who beats up Drew?"

"Drew does," Petersen said.

"What? Drew beats himself up?"

"Yeah, when he realizes that he can pin it on Damon, he hits himself in the face, repeatedly." I studied Petersen's face, looking for some hint that he was joking. It became clear that he wasn't. Petersen continued, "After beating himself up, he gets Josh to say it was Damon. Josh agrees, because he knows this means he'll get to live with his father." Petersen snapped his fingers and pointed at me before saying, "That would explain why Drew didn't leave any marks on his attacker. Well, in a way, he did."

"Not to burst your bubble, but there's one thing you forgot. Drew is right handed."

"You're right handed," Petersen said, gesturing toward me. "Act like you're punching yourself in the face." I slowly moved my right fist toward my face. "Stop right there," Petersen said as I held my fist near my face. "See, being right handed, you would naturally leave bruises on the right side of your face. That's where Drew's bruises were."

I dropped my fist down to my side. "You can't honestly believe that Drew beat himself up."

"Well, I'm not saying that he did. I'm only saying that it's a possibility. I still think it was Steve." I shook my head in disagreement. "Listen, this case is really pretty simple. We have Josh and Drew saying it was Damon. So, it's either Damon or it's someone who the boys want to protect. And the evidence says it's not Damon."

"But, that's what I still don't get. Why would they want to protect their attacker?"

"Either out of obligation or fear, I don't know. What I do know is it's someone Drew couldn't bring himself to hit. I'm sorry, but the only person that fits that description is his dad."

"For the last time, it's not Steve. He wouldn't have touched his sons. I know him."

"Maybe that's the problem."

"Excuse me?"

"Robert, I have long admired your intuition and detective skills. But, on this case, a pretty straight forward one at that, you seem to be baffled. And I can't help but think it's because you lack objectivity with the key suspects." Frustrated, I got up from the table, leaving a $10 bill. "Hey. Where are you going?"

"To the school, to prove you wrong," I said over my shoulder, as I headed toward the coffee shop exit.

It was about ten thirty when I sat down on the bench in the football bleachers. The wind began to pick up on this chilly Fall day. I was watching Coach Fox blow his whistle and yell at some kids. When he started walking toward the bleachers, I walked down to meet him.

"You've taken a sudden interest in high school P.E.?" Coach Fox said.

"No, I came to give you some news about Percy's alleged breaking and entering."

"I'll be back in a minute!" Coach Fox shouted at the group of kids on the other side of the field. He motioned to me to follow him. He led me to his office and took a seat behind his desk. As I took a seat on one of the hard, wooden chairs, he asked me, "So, what's the news you have about Percy?"

"Well, I talked to the school and found out who witnessed Percy break into the snack shack. It was Josh Granger."

The coach slumped back in his chair and tilted his head slightly. "You're joking?"

"No joke," I said, shaking my head.

He leaned back in his chair and rubbed his chin. "Now, why do you think Josh would make up a story like that?"

"Well, I don't think Josh is lying," I said. "But seeing how Percy is your star quarterback, I can understand that you would want to protect him." I leaned forward and looked into Coach Fox's eyes. "The question is how far you'd go to protect Percy. Would you beat Josh up to force him to change what he says he witnessed?"

Coach Fox froze for a moment. "I never laid a hand on that boy and I resent the accusation." He thumped his desk with his right hand before grabbing the school's yearbook. He opened it to the page featuring last year's junior varsity team. "I love these kids. I'd never hurt them, especially Drew."

"I know Drew. He loves his brother and he would have come after just about anyone if they hurt Josh."

"That's right," Coach Fox said. "If someone beat Josh up, Drew would have sought payback, physically. Do you see any marks on me?"

"He wouldn't have touched you though. Not if it meant he would get tossed from the football team. You mind taking off your gloves?"

Coach Fox slowly pulled off his gloves. "I have nothing to hide." He showed off both hands, palms up and down. I leaned closer to get a better look. Both of his hands were unmarked. "I believe someone owes me an apology," he said, punctuated by pounding his fist on the open yearbook.

"That's the second time you hit your desk with your right fist," I said in deep thought. "You're right handed, aren't you?"

"Yeah, so what?"

I still kept my eyes peeled on Coach Fox's right fist. "I'm so sorry. I thought you were the one that was so upset with Josh for ratting on Percy." My eyes continued to widen in shock as I looked at his fist.

He noticed my expression. "Now what's the matter?"

"Your fist, lift it please." A confused Coach Fox slowly lifted his fist off the yearbook. "Well, you're right about one thing coach. Once Drew found out Josh had been beaten up, he retaliated, big time." I pointed to where his fist had been resting. "That's Percy Brown in that picture, isn't it?"

"Yeah, so what?"

I didn't answer him. I shook my head and stared at the picture, which showed Percy throwing a pass, left-handed.

The Emotion
of Henry Burrows

Ex-inspector Henry Burrows looked at the picture of a beautiful, smiling, seventeen-year-old girl and a tear dropped from his eye. In his thirty years in the homicide division, Henry had seen his share of gruesome murders, with victims often taken in the prime of their lives. No matter how shocking or how tragic, he was always stoically analytical and determined. Nothing seemed to ever emotionally rattle old Henry Burrows. But, this time was different. This time, homicide had hit home and the victim was his seventeen-year-old granddaughter.

It was Saturday morning, about sixteen hours since the police had delivered the awful news. Henry wiped his eyes as he slowly walked down the hallway to Lt. James Harper's office. At sixty-nine years old, Henry had been retired for six years. When he was working, James worked for him and, over the years, they had become friends.

Henry knocked on his door as he peered through the glass wall. James, who was on the phone, immediately waved him in. As James finished his phone call, Henry stood, waiting patiently. James had a squarish face and a full head of black hair with just a touch of gray.

James hung up the phone and walked over to give Henry a hug. "I'm so sorry. Jennifer was a great girl."

"You said you have the boy you think is responsible for Jennifer's death in custody. We need to make sure he pays for what he did," Henry said, his eyes welling up.

"Please, have a seat," James said, as both men sat down in adjacent chairs.

"We can't let him get away with saying he was temporarily insane."

"Right now, he's not saying anything. His parents made sure he won't talk until his lawyer gets here."

"Tell me everything you know about this kid."

James picked up a file. "He's eighteen years old, only child, well-to-do family, mom's a nurse, father's a CPA. The kid's record is clean. According to school officials, he's not a loner, but not one of the popular kids either. It's kind of surprising. This is not your typical profile for a mass murderer."

"You can't always judge a book by its cover," Henry said. "There have been a few massacres on high school and college campuses from seemingly well adjusted kids. This boy murdered my granddaughter and three of her classmates."

"Yeah, but this is different," James cautioned. "This wasn't a rage-filled, heat of passion killing. It was meticulously planned and calculated."

"The question I have is 'Why?'. Why did he target Jennifer? Why her boyfriend? Their parents looked at the school's yearbook. Neither parent recognized the boy."

"If you are looking for why, I think only one person knows that and he's not talking."

"Take me to his cell," Henry said. "I want to talk to him."

"I don't think that's such a…"

"James please, just let me talk to him for a few minutes."

James paused for a moment before giving in and escorting Henry to holding cell #4.

Emotions consumed Henry as he looked at the boy behind the bars. Henry's heartbeat quickened and his stomach turned with disgust. He hated the boy inside this cell. He moved a couple of steps closer. He grabbed the cell bars with both hands and stuck his nose between the bars to get a better look at the boy. James remained a few steps behind Henry.

Seeing he had a visitor, the boy sat up in his bed. He had short, blond hair and a youthful face. As Henry studied him, his posture portrayed confidence, bordering on arrogance. However, his darting, blue eyes suggested a deep fear.

"May I help you?" the boy asked sarcastically.

Henry gripped the cell bars a little tighter as he asked, "Are you Mark Davidson?"

The boy nodded before asking, "Who are you?"

"My name's Henry Burrows."

Mark looked at James and then back at Henry. "Are you cops deaf? I've already told you I'm not talking to the police."

"I'm not the police. I'm Jennifer's grandfather. The girl you murdered." Henry flashed a piercing glare that seemed to shoot straight through a stunned Mark. "I just want to know one thing. Why did you do it? What did Jennifer do to deserve this?"

Mark stood up and walked up to the cell bars and right in front of Henry, who stood his ground. James remained alert, in case Mark became aggressive. "I did not kill your granddaughter. I didn't kill any of the other kids either."

"You should be able to tell from my gray hair that I wasn't born yesterday. Now, we both know what you did. I'm only asking you why. Why did you inject a syringe of arsenic into my granddaughter?"

"Damn it!" Mark shouted as he hit the cell bars with his open right hand. James took a step forward, but Henry immediately waved him back. "I told you! I didn't do it!"

Henry looked at Mark with disdain. "You'd better watch that temper. It makes your guilt more evident." Mark simmered with frustration. He locked his fingers together as they rested on top of his head. Henry continued, "Perhaps you can explain why the authorities found you with four dead bodies of your classmates. Your fingerprints and only your fingerprints were all over the murder weapons."

Mark closed his eyes for a moment before saying, "All I can tell you is that it wasn't me. I swear."

"Oh, you swear? The authorities found you alone on a boat with four dead bodies. So, tell me. How did he get away?"

Mark's forehead wrinkled as he dropped both arms to his side. "How did *who* get away?"

"Don't play games with me. You claim you didn't do it. So, I asked you how the guy who did it got away."

Mark paused for a few seconds. "I really shouldn't be talking to you. Just leave me alone," Mark said before walking back to the bed.

Henry squinted as he tilted his head slightly. He knew something wasn't right. He just didn't know what.

"Well, that was a waste of time," James said as they re-entered his office.

"Maybe, maybe not," Henry said, stroking his chin.

"Other than saying he didn't do it, he didn't tell us anything."

"Oh no, he told us much more than that. When I asked him how the murderer got away, he didn't know who I was referring to. I expected him to make up some story about a helicopter or a boat, but that's not what happened." Henry wagged his finger. "That tells me something."

James flashed a perplexed look as his phone rang. He picked it up and listened for a few moments before hanging up. "It seems that Mark's parents have arrived, with their lawyer. I need to take care of this."

"Go ahead," Henry said. "I just need to look at the police report on the crime scene and access to your computer."

"You got it," James said, before handing him a file and heading out the door.

About an hour later, James returned to his office. "I'm sorry about the wait. Shortly after his lawyer got here, Mark was ready to talk. And you won't believe his story. He sai…"

"He said that Robert Green murdered the other three victims before committing suicide."

James' jaw dropped. "My God. How did you know that?"

"Because in the last hour, I figured out what happened." Speechless, James waited for an explanation. "There were five people on the boat, Mark and four of his dead classmates. The question is, who was the last to die? Susan Tolliver, another victim on the boat, could not have been the last one alive because she couldn't have committed suicide by stabbing herself in the back. It's theoretically possible that Jennifer could have injected herself with the syringe, but her body was found in the bedroom and the syringe was found all the way in the front of the boat in the control room."

"Why didn't you suspect Max? He died the same way as Robert, taking arsenic orally."

"I suppose it's possible Max poisoned Robert, stabbed Susan in the back and then injected Jennifer with the syringe before drinking arsenic to commit suicide to frame Mark. But, Max has the same problem as Jennifer. He was found in the bedroom far away from the control room which is, according to forensics, where the glass that showed traces of arsenic that Max drank from."

"So, you think this Robert kid is the murderer?"

"I suspected him, so I looked into his background. His family owned the boat and the revolver, which was onboard.

Forensics couldn't find what he drank the arsenic from, but he was found in the control room. He could have drank from a glass and thrown it overboard before collapsing. So, the evidence shows he could have committed suicide. I just don't know why he would have."

"According to Mark, he had leukemia. Perhaps he was going to die anyway."

Henry paused to think. "Did Mark have any idea why Robert did this?"

"He said that Robert told him, just before committing suicide, that he did it for revenge."

"Revenge for what?"

"He didn't give any further details. Wait a minute, you really believe Mark? You think he's innocent?"

"Yes," Henry said, nodding slowly.

"But we have him as the only person alive on a boat with four dead bodies. His fingerprints were the only ones on the knife and the syringe. He also had prints on the revolver."

"There was no evidence that the revolver was even shot."

"No, but maybe Mark used it to force Robert to drink the arsenic and Mark threw the glass out to sea."

"Good theory, but think about it. If he planned all this out so meticulously, why did he leave his fingerprints on everything? Why didn't he have a way to escape as opposed to calling the Coast Guard to find him with four dead bodies?"

James stared at Henry for a few moments before shrugging. "I can't answer that."

Henry stared at James for a moment. "As much as it pains me to say this, you gotta let him go."

"I've got Jensen in there playing bad cop to see if we can shake him."

"That won't do any good. Just cut him loose."

Before James could respond, another officer burst in the room. "We need you now! There was an altercation in the interrogation room."

James and Henry raced out of the office and down the hallway where they met Officer Jensen, whose lip was bleeding.

"That punk hit me," the officer said to James. "I'm pressing charges."

While James ushered Jensen into a nearby holding room, Henry asked a middle-aged man in a suit, "Are you Mark's attorney?"

"Yes," the man said.

"I'm a retired police officer and the grandfather of one of the victims. I don't think your client murdered anyone. Can we talk? I think you'll want to hear what I have to say."

"Sure," Mark's attorney said as they walked back to the interrogation room.

"This is ridiculous," Mark said, seated at the table in the interrogation room. "Why is everyone treating me like some monster? I didn't kill anyone."

"And I believe you. You're no murderer and I can prove it," Henry said.

Mark took a few moments to realize what Henry said. Henry took a seat at the table. "You're serious?" Mark asked him.

"Dead serious," Henry said. "You should not be punished for anything that happened on that boat. I'm confident the police will share my belief. They won't charge you for murder."

Mark collapsed on the table in relief. "He didn't outsmart me. I beat him. I beat Luke."

Henry's forehead wrinkled. "Luke? Who's Luke?"

"Oh that's just a nickname I used for Robert, the creep who murdered your granddaughter."

"You called him Luke?" Henry said in deep thought. "You did that because you knew he had leukemia. That's terrible."

"He deserved it. Look, when do you think the police will let me go?"

"They aren't going to let you go," Henry said.

"What? But, you just said..."

"I said that the police wouldn't charge you for murder, but you assaulted a police officer. You're going to do time for that."

"That's not fair. If the police didn't wrongfully arrest me, I never would have hit that cop."

"That may be true, but you're still responsible for your actions. You said earlier that Robert told you that he acted out of revenge. So, if you didn't tease Robert so ruthlessly, maybe he wouldn't have murdered Jennifer and her two classmates."

"I had nothing to do with Jennifer's death," Mark said sternly.

"I know," Henry said, rising. A swarm of mixed emotions came over Henry as he realized the investigation into his most personal case ever was coming to a close. "Like I said, you're only responsible for your actions. Because you hit a cop, you will be going to jail." Henry started for the door.

"This is not fair!" Mark shouted at Henry.

Henry stopped just inside the door and slowly turned around. "I've lost a granddaughter, so don't talk to me about fairness!" Henry paused for a moment, trying to control his emotion. "You should use your time in jail to reflect on how you have treated people, including how you treated Robert. If it makes you change how you treat people in the future, then there would be at least one good thing that came out of this terrible tragedy."

About the Stories

WARNING: This section should not be read until AFTER you have read all of the stories in this book. In this section, I do give away some of the clues, climax, and conclusion of the stories.

In life, it seems we are bombarded with things we don't need or want. If we watch our favorite sit-com, we have to put up with the commercials. If we want to fly, airport security, delays, and substandard food are all part of the experience. My goal as a mystery writer is to give the readers only what they really want and need…nothing more, nothing less.

So, what makes a great story? Yes, a strong opening. Sure, being able to build suspense during the middle. And, of course, a powerful ending which will leave the readers happy they made the time and emotional investment in the story. Equally important however, is to minimize the fluff, and keep up the pace of the story.

I believe in extremely tightly written stories. I go through many rounds of re-writes, always asking myself if every paragraph, sentence, and even word is truly necessary. If I have to think about it for too long, it's deleted from the story.

In the end, my goal is for the reader to feel he has a "page turner" that he can't put down. To me, that's the biggest compliment a mystery writer can ever receive.

Eric J. Lee

Murder in a Snow Covered Town

Sometimes, less is more and I think this story demonstrates that. I slashed this story, previously called *Disappearing Act*, by removing one third of it. I got rid of unnecessary prose and dialog, but retained the heart of the story. In the rewrite process, I also rounded out some of the characters. The biggest character change was to Brian. Clearly, he still has flaws (and needs to for the ending of the story to work), but he was no longer written as an evil character.

This story takes the reader through a kidnapping, child abuse and finally murder. They are left to guess along with the narrator as to who is behind all of this. A lot of my stories revolve around a murder. This one is driven by a kidnapping. The reader is left to wonder who kidnapped the innocent Cindy, whether she would be found, and whether she would be found alive. When the murder happens in the middle of the story, it raises the suspicion that someone is trying to conceal the kidnapper's identity "no matter what." Anything, as Riley says, "to save the town".

With events snowballing against Riley, the image of a snowball going down a hill caused me to change the story's title. In the end, this story is about what someone did, albeit unsuccessfully, to protect his "family" as opposed to the disappearance of a young girl.

I used the actual weather in this story to mirror Riley's snowball metaphor. As Riley gets himself deeper and deeper into this mess, the snowstorm gets worse.

About the Stories

Painful Decision

I wanted this story to work on two levels. First, to tell the heart-wrenching story of a dog-owner making the painful decision to euthanize an old dog with health problems, and second, to challenge the reader to figure out that Johnny is the narrator's pet, not son. In the end, my hope is to fool most readers into thinking that Johnny is his son rather than his pet. By doing that, I hope the story dramatically demonstrates the narrator's love and devotion, and reflects the special place dogs have in our society.

As I wrote this, I had to decide how many and what kind of clues I would give that hinted at Johnny being a dog. Straightforward clues included describing Johnny as "a best friend", playing off the phrase man's best friend. I opted to use the flashback of "when I would throw the ball with him in the park", but decided against using the flashback to "our long walks in the park."

More subtle clues included Johnny lying on his stomach in the doctor's office (unusual for a human) and Dr. Roberts sighing and rolling his eyes when the narrator asked him to lower his voice, as if Johnny could understand what they were saying.

I used a writing "trick" to instill in the readers mind that Johnny was a child. In the second paragraph, I mention "my wife was on a business trip". This plants a picture in the reader's mind of a nuclear family. That conjures up the image of a child, as opposed to a dog, to round out this family.

I Will Live Before I Die

I originally wrote this story over twenty years ago when I was in high school and, though I recently re-wrote it, the concept

189

of a dying student seeking revenge on students from different cliques comes from the original story written long ago.

Telling the story from the perspective of a premeditated murderer is a challenging task. In general, the reader wants to root for the narrator. That was next to impossible in this story. I did want the reader to be able to get in the mind of the narrator to be able to understand why he would resort to violence.

To further the motive for violence, I had to work on rounding out the narrator's adversaries in the rewrite process. The two characters I changed the most were Jennifer and Mark. Quick question: What is the opposite of love? Most say it's hate. I think it's complete apathy. And apathy is how Jennifer returns the love of the narrator. She simply doesn't care about him or his feelings. To her, he's basically irrelevant. On the other hand, in Mark's eyes, the narrator is very relevant. I wanted to play up the intense competition between Mark and the narrator to the point that it was clearly an unhealthy rivalry. Most readers felt that Mark's usage of the nickname of "Luke" conveyed that he went "over the line".

When writing this story, I wanted to make sure the characters met their demise in a special, symbolic way. The girl who gossips ruthlessly was stabbed in the back. The girl who took advantage of the narrator's affection dies in his arms. The strong, tough guy was the first and easiest for the narrator to murder. And the brilliant rival is outsmarted in the end.

Murder in the Suburbs

I am always looking for innovative ways to tell a suspense story. For a long time, I wanted to tell a story from the perspective of the murderer, without the reader realizing he was the culprit. The challenge is that the reader sees everything the narrator does. Thus, to pull this feat off, I had to drop the reader into the story after the murder. This is a little awkward, so when I came up with the idea to make it appear that the murder happened later, I felt I had the makings of a great story.

I used the wife's call to the radio show to establish that she was alive during the telling of the story. This also pointed suspicion away from the narrator because he couldn't have been in two places once.

I had a decision to make about how long I wanted this story to be. I could have gone with a longer version that would have developed a red herring to implicate the sheriff or a newly developed character. However, I opted for the shorter, faster-paced, story, which only has two other suspects, Hal and Adam. And when the time of death is established to be earlier, only Adam remains a suspect other than the narrator.

Since I'm telling the story from the perspective of the murderer, I must remain true to that reality. That's why at the beginning, shortly after the narrator has actually killed his wife, the narrator is consumed with his thoughts and his friend notices something is wrong. He asks, "What's the matter with you?" I also have a little fun with this reality. Upon arriving at the crime scene, I write in reference to the narrator: "What's going on?" I asked, even though I already knew. Finally, it's not just what the narrator says that must ring true. All of the narrator's inner thoughts and emotions must be consistent with the fact that he is the murderer without giving that away to the reader. All in all, it was a fun, but rather challenging task.

Corner of the Living Room

They say a picture is worth a thousand words. So are "flash fiction" stories. This story is one of several of my stories of a thousand words or less. When I get an interesting but simple concept, I enjoy writing stories of this length. They take only six to eight hours to write on the first draft. The re-writing process, however, can take weeks or even months before I'm happy with the finished product.

This is an extremely short story given that it has five characters. There's the narrator, Evan, the two police officers, and Monica. Each of the supporting characters has a specific purpose as the suspense builds. Ideally, the reader does not realize Evan is a character on television until the last couple of lines of the story.

The clues to this story are more subtle than some of my other stories. The narrator sinks into the couch as if she is watching television. Evan never addresses the narrator or talks directly toward her. The strongest clue is when the narrator picks up the remote control and points it at Evan to silence him.

I thought about this story when I realized how we can be drawn into a good television show or movie. We can grow to love or hate a character even though we know he's not real. Very good characters, heroes as well as villains, can take on a life of its own.

Murder is a Deadly Game

When I got the idea for this story, I was very excited. The original premise was for an escaped prisoner to gather together the people who had a hand in sentencing him together for the purpose of staging his death. What better witnesses to his death to swear that any manhunt should be called off.

Tension rises immediately as the parties at the mansion begin to look familiar, but no one can quite remember why. Then, a hostage situation ensues before the staged death. The challenge was where to take the story from there. I wanted the reader to understand what happened, but how could I do that?

About the Stories

My original story had the escaped prisoner sending a letter to the police, years later, bragging about his hoax, but it didn't feel right to me. With over ten years on the shelf, I finally got an ending I was satisfied with and rewrote the story.

The first change was to make the prisoner innocent of the original crime, framed by the detective. Then, the detective would hunt down the escaped prisoner. In the end, the story addressed the concept of success and reputation. The detective believed that his reputation made him, by definition, a success and allowed him to be able to do whatever he wanted. His downfall was his overconfidence, since he could not resist bragging about his accomplishments to his long-time rival. Ultimately, it costs him his freedom, reputation, and the "cat and mouse game" with his old rival.

Roadblock on Memory Lane

The concept of being economical with words is never more true than in my poetry. This poem was a scant thousand words. Each of my books includes a rhyming poem, but this is the only one I've ever written with in-depth dialog and developing plot. This was really a story that happened to be in a poem format. It takes the reader through an investigation of murder with two prime suspects, Mark and Sue. The major twist here is not only that the narrator is the murderer, but he doesn't know it. Because he suffers from amnesia, he wonders along with the reader who is behind this. Line by line, the narrator gets a clearer picture of what is going on. Eventually, the narrator and the reader realize the horrific truth.

When I got this idea, I thought about writing it in the format of a long story. However, this idea, although fresh and powerful, seemed more suited to a short, hard-hitting format.

Although I began writing rhyming poetry long before I ever wrote my first mystery story, I'm no longer a fan of that style. At times, I find it frustrating and slow. I can literally spend thirty minutes writing two lines. However, once complete and I am satisfied, the poetry flows and does not feel forced, I am very proud of the work. I'll never change my trade to being a poet, but I kind of like to moonlight as one every now and then.

Love Hurts

I brought back one of my favorite narrators, private eye Robert Douglas, for this story. It was interesting writing a mystery story that had nothing to do with a murder. Instead, it was simply a story about who beat up a freshman high school kid and why.

Straying away from murder and mayhem, I was nervous that I wouldn't gain the automatic interest that comes with an impending death. I put a lot of effort into building suspense in the first few pages with Steve's impassioned plea to protect his boys.

From there, this is character-driven story with many different characters, having many different motivations and goals. In the midst of deceit, and secrecy, the private eye and the reader are left to sort it all out.

I tried a different "reveal" at the end of this story. Because the narrator suspects other characters, the foundations were set for the how and why someone may have beaten up Drew and Josh. Therefore, I was able to reveal the culprit was Percy Brown without any further discussion. I think it makes for a shorter, and thus more powerful, ending.

About the Stories

Emotion of Henry Burrows

Ever since I finished writing *I Will Live before I Die*, I wondered how I could creatively write a sequel. I wanted to make sure any sequel would not take away from the original story. Then, I thought of a twist to write the story from the perspective of a different narrator. One of the charms of this sequel was that "ah ha" moment when the reader realizes this is a continuation of *I Will Live before I Die*. I intended this to happen about one third of the way through the story.

The story explores the concept of responsibility for your actions, even when put in extreme situations. Robert, the narrator in *I Will Live before I Die*, was put in an extreme situation as he suffered from leukemia. No matter how sad his situation is, he is responsible for "playing the cards he was dealt". Mark is held to same standard, as he must pay for his violent temper when pushed heavily by the police.

The ending of this story completes the mission of the narrator in *I Will Live Before I Die*. His original goal was to change the behavior of his four classmates. He decided to kill them because he felt he could not change them. At Henry's urging in this story, we are left with the hope that the only survivor, Mark, will actually change his ways.

Other short story collections by this author:

This book features ten short mystery and suspense stories sure to entertain, surprise, and intrigue the reader. In the short story, *Murder in a Country Town*, the narrator, an avid hunter, is obsessed with killing the sheriff of a small country town. What is at the root of the narrator's hatred? In a high stakes game of cat and mouse, exactly who has the upper hand? Will the narrator be successful, or will the hunter become the hunted?

In another story, a young accountant is working late in the office on a Friday night. Living alone, he calls home to leave himself a simple reminder message. Instead of hearing his answering machine, someone answers the phone. When he asks to speak to himself, the familiar voice says, "Speaking." He quickly comes to a startling realization. The voice sounds identical to his.

For more information about the author and his stories, please visit his official website at www.ericleestories.com

Other short story collections by this author:

This book features nine short mystery and suspense stories. In the short story, *Murder in a Coastal Town*, a homicide detective, is overcome with grief at the murder of his eight-year-old son. The only witness to the murder is his eleven-year-old daughter. How does he extract detailed information about the murder from a witness who is desperately trying to forget? Will the detective ever be able to catch the murderer and what emotional price is he willing to pay?

In another story, the reader is dropped in the jury box of a high profile murder case. The senator's husband could be facing the death penalty. Private eye and jury member Robert Douglas is used to solving cases, but how will he be able to convince eleven strangers to adopt his perspective on the case.

For more information about the author and his stories, please visit his official website at www.ericleestories.com

Other novels by this author:

Trying to Win at Love tells the funny and inspiring story of a new tennis captain pressed into running a local team because "there's no one else." As his own expectations for success rise, the rookie captain begins to equate wins as validation from his players and competitors. His troubles, which aren't limited to the court, soon mount as quickly as his victories. A group of colorful characters and extraordinary events teach him valuable lessons about winning on the court and in life.

For more information about the author and his stories, please visit his official website at www.ericleestories.com.

Other novels by this author:

In this humorous and inspirational sequel to the novel *Trying to Win at Love*, the narrator copes with several stinging losses. Faced with new challenges, he discovers that old approaches don't always provide the solution. Without the comfort and familiarity of the past, he struggles in his attempt to find a new team and mend a broken heart. In the process, he learns a lot about himself and life as he once again tries to win at love.

For more information about the author and his stories, please visit his official website at www.ericleestories.com.

www.ingramcontent.com/pod-product-compliance
Lightning Source LLC
Chambersburg PA
CBHW051509170626
46811CB00002B/719

* 9 7 8 0 9 6 7 4 4 7 6 3 6 *